ABBY AND THE SECRET SOCIETY

At last, Kristy stumbled across a clue—literally! She was walking through the dining room when she tripped and almost fell. She had put down a hand to catch herself, and now she noticed that a corner of the old, stained, brown carpet wasn't completely tacked down.

"No wonder I nearly fell," she muttered to herself. Then, just out of curiosity, she flipped up the carpet to see what kind of flooring lay underneath. It turned out to be wooden planks, but that wasn't what made her draw a sudden breath. It was the stain she saw, across the corner of the flooring. A distinct, deep purplish-red stain that looked a little like writing. Kristy peered more closely at it, but couldn't work out what it said, or if it said anything at all. She sat back on her heels to think, and a beautiful, gold-framed mirror caught her eye. "That's it!" she exclaimed.

Also available in the Babysitters Club Mysteries series:

1 Stacey and the Missing Ring
2 Beware, Dawn!
3 Mallory and the Ghost Cat
4 Kristy and the Missing Child
5 Mary Anne and the Secret in the Attic
6 The Mystery at Claudia's House
7 Dawn and the Disappearing Dogs
8 Jessi and the Jewel Thieves
9 Kristy and the Haunted Mansion
11 Claudia and the Mystery at the Museum
12 Dawn and the Surfer Ghost
13 Mary Anne and the Library Mystery
14 Stacey and the Mystery at the Mall
15 Kristy and the Vampires
16 Claudia and the Clue in the Photograph
17 Dawn and the Halloween Mystery
18 Stacey and the Mystery of the Empty House
19 Kristy and the Missing Fortune
20 Mary Anne and the Zoo Mystery
21 Claudia and the Recipe for Danger
22 Stacey and the Haunted Masquerade

Look out for:

24 Mary Anne and the Silent Witness
25 Kristy and the Middle School Vandal

ABBY AND THE
SECRET SOCIETY

Ann M. Martin

*The author gratefully acknowledges
Ellen Miles
for her help in
preparing this manuscript.*

Scholastic Children's Books,
Commonwealth House, 1–19 New Oxford Street,
London WC1A 1NU, UK
a division of Scholastic Ltd
London ~ New York ~ Toronto ~ Sydney ~ Auckland

First published in the US by Scholastic Inc., 1996
First published in the UK by Scholastic Ltd, 1996

Text Copyright © Ann M. Martin, 1996
THE BABYSITTERS CLUB is a registered trademark of
Scholastic Inc.

ISBN 0 590 13893 6

All rights reserved

Typeset by Rowland Phototypesetting Ltd,
Bury St Edmunds, Suffolk
Printed by Cox & Wyman Ltd, Reading, Berks.

10 9 8 7 6 5 4 3 2 1

1st CHAPTER

"I'm sorry. I really am. It breaks my heart. But we have to face reality. I love you, but I just can't go out with you," I said.

I giggled until I began laughing. Then I leaned back against the wall and sighed.

I bet you're wondering what the guy thought.

Well, there was no guy. The speech I'd made was directed to a pair of skis.

"You've really gone around the bend this time, Abigail Stevenson," I told myself. I shook my head. It's one thing talking to yourself, but talking to sporting goods is really pushing it. And the thing was, it hadn't just been the skis. I'd been standing in front of the hall cupboard Mum lets me use for all my sports equipment, chatting to my ice skates, my baseball glove, my running shoes and even my tennis racket.

1

Maybe I should explain. It's February. Doesn't that make everything clear?

Well, for me it does. February is my least favourite month of the year. February is just so—*Februaryish*. It has absolutely nothing going for it, unless you're a big fan of Valentine's Day, or of the winter sales. I couldn't care less about either. But one thing I do care about is being active. I love being outside, working up a sweat. I play football in the autumn, and softball in the summer. I bike, I run, I ski, I play tennis. Sports aren't my whole life; I have plenty of other interests. But in February, I miss sports most of all. It's always gloomy and grey in February, and it's too cold for some things (such as running, or tennis), and often too warm for others (such as skiing).

The only good thing about February, for me, is that there isn't much pollen floating around in the air. Pollen is The Enemy, as far as my respiratory system is concerned. I am outrageously allergic to the stuff. I have other enemies, too, such as animal hair and dust, but pollen is the worst because it's everywhere and you can't avoid it. So, as long as my asthma doesn't start early, I usually breathe easily during February. But apart from that, the month is basically useless.

So that's why I told my tennis racket

that it would have to wait for me, and my softball glove that I adored it but that it didn't make sense for us to be together just then. I'd vowed to go out with my skates "one day" (if the pond ever froze over again) and promised my running shoes a date in the near future.

Fortunately nobody observed me playing out these crazy little love scenes. This was one time I was thankful to be home alone. I'm home alone a lot of the time. That's because my family consists of just me and two other people: my twin sister Anna, and our mum.

The three of us moved into this house not long ago, after my mum was given a big promotion at work. We used to live in a nice house on Long Island (that's in New York), but when Mum was promoted she decided we could afford to move to an even nicer, bigger house in Stoneybrook, Connecticut. Mum commutes to work in New York City, which is an hour-long train journey away. I didn't mind the move much. I think it's fun to shake things up and bring change into your life.

Good change, that is. Not horrible, sudden, painful change. I know about that kind of change, too. I went through it four years ago when my dad died in a car crash. That changed our family for ever, and—

And I really don't want to talk about it. It still hurts too much. I'd rather tell you more about my family and me. First of all, Anna and I are identical twins. We're both thirteen, but Anna is about eight minutes older than me; she was born first. She loves reminding me to respect my "elders". We have brown eyes (short-sighted ones—we both wear contact lenses and glasses interchangeably), and sort of pointy faces. And while we do look a lot alike, nobody has trouble telling us apart. That's partly because I wear my dark, curly hair long and Anna wears hers short.

But it's also because we're so different. Anna would never talk to a cupboardful of athletic equipment. Cupboardful of musical instruments, maybe. I can't imagine what you could say to a violin, but Anna would know. Anna is Miss Violin. She knows everything about the instrument, as she's been playing it practically for ever. Music is her life. Most of her friends are from orchestras or other groups she plays in. She has private lessons and practises for hours every day. She's really good, I suppose. I wouldn't know for sure, since as far as musical taste goes, I'm more into Motown than Mozart.

So Anna's dedicated to her music, and my mum's dedicated to her job. (She's a

4

real workaholic, especially since my dad died.) And me? I'm dedicated to having fun. I like things to happen, and if that means I have to make them happen, well, that's OK by me. I like meeting people and going places and doing things, and I hate—absolutely *hate*—being bored.

And that afternoon, I was definitely bored. In fact, I was so bored that I actually (gasp!) decided to go up to my room and start on my maths homework. (I usually scramble through my maths homework during tutor time. Procrastination is my middle name.) After one last, lingering glance at my skis, I closed the cupboard door and trudged up the stairs.

I'd only just made it through Problem 4A (out of twenty-five) when I heard the front door open and close. I flew down the stairs. "Anna! You're home!" I cried, flinging my arms around my sister.

Anna took a surprised step backwards and raised her eyebrows at me. We are not normally a demonstrative family. "Hello, Abby," she said, putting down her violin case as she unbuttoned her coat.

"I am so glad to see you," I said.

"I noticed," she replied. "And I wondered why. Do I owe you money or something?"

"No, of course not. It's just that I've been so bored, and now that you're home we can do something together. Like . . . like," I paused to think, and then I snapped my fingers. "Like make a terrific dinner, to surprise Mum. She promised to be home early tonight, but I bet she's planning to order pizza or something."

I was babbling away so fast that I hardly noticed Anna shaking her head. "I can't," she said, when I finally calmed down. "I promised Lydia I'd transpose this Telemann concerto so she could play it on her clarinet." She pulled a piece of music out of a folder and showed it to me.

I barely glanced at it. "Telemann, Schmelemann," I said. "Please, Anna? Just this once, and I promise I'll never ask you for anything again. Please? Please?" I got down on my knees and made the silliest, most pleading face I could.

Anna laughed. "You really are desperate, aren't you?" she said. "OK. Why don't you go and find a recipe while I change?"

"Yahoo!" I cried and gave her another big hug. Then I charged into the kitchen and started pulling cookbooks off the shelf.

Twenty minutes later, the kitchen was a total wreck. My mother always says I cook using the "every-pot-in-the-house" method, and she's pretty much on target. I tell her that I learned it from her, which is also on target. She cooks that way because that's how professional chefs do it. They never have to clean up after themselves—the lowly under-chefs do that—so they just make all the mess they want.

The reason Mum cooks like a professional chef is that she spent some time studying to be one, at a famous cookery school called the Culinary Institute of America. I remember when she went to pastry classes, and brought home the most amazing fruit tarts and puff pastries every week. She was really happy then—and so were we, since we got to eat all her class projects.

That was before Dad was in the accident. After that, Mum never went to a cookery class again.

So! Where was I? Right. In the kitchen with Anna, making a big mess. We had a great time. We made a fabulous pasta dish, with sun-dried tomatoes and basil, as well as a batch of very garlicky garlic bread and a huge salad. We talked a lot while we cooked. Anna told me how shy she feels with this guy she likes (just as a friend) in our school orchestra. I complained to Anna about how the BSC hasn't had much business lately, because everybody's staying at home. (The BSC—Babysitters Club—is a club I was asked to join when I moved here. The

7

name is self-explanatory, but I'll tell you more about the club some other time.) We talked a little about Mum, and how hard she's been working lately. And we commiserated about how much study time we have to put in over the next two months learning Hebrew for becoming a Bat Mitzvah. (That's a big Jewish celebration for girls when they reach thirteen.)

But we also laughed a lot, and threw vegetables at each other, and teased each other about the garlic breath we were going to have later that night. And, miracle of miracles, at exactly 6:45 Mum walked in through the door, home early, just as she'd promised.

We had a terrific dinner together. And I even had fun clearing up afterwards, with Mum's help. Not only that, but I finished my maths homework that night.

I should have felt satisfied and happy as I lay in bed later, waiting for sleep to come. But guess what? I didn't. Instead, I found myself dreading the rest of February. It may be the shortest month, but it feels like the longest to me. I needed something to do, something to focus on, something to make the rest of those twenty-eight days fly by.

That's why I perked up the next morning during tutor time, when an announcement came over the public address system. The announcement was about the new SMS (Stoneybrook Middle School) jobs noticeboard. Hmm. An interesting part-time job might be exactly what I was looking for.

I made my way to the noticeboard as soon as tutor time ended. Quickly, I ran my eyes over the listings, ignoring the ads for babysitters, dog-walkers and newspaper-deliverers—all the usual part-time jobs. "Boring, boring, boring," I muttered. Then I spotted it. "Yes!" I said softly to myself, pumping my fist. "This is it." I read through the ad carefully. The Greenbrook Club, which sounded like your basic country club, with golf and tennis and a pool, was looking for students to help with pre-season painting, cleaning, decoration and even childcare (for the children of the other workers, I assumed). The pay was excellent.

Suddenly, I felt a lot more hopeful about the rest of February. I couldn't wait to tell all my BSC friends about Greenbrook's ad. I had a feeling I wasn't the only one with the late-winter blues.

2nd
CHAPTER

They say first impressions are lasting.

They also say that you can't judge a book by its cover.

Who are They, anyway? And why don't They pull their act together and stop contradicting Themselves?

Actually, They are right on both counts. First impressions do tell a lot about a person. On the other hand, there are some things you can't know about someone until you've spent a little more time with them.

I was thinking about all of this as I sat in Claudia's room that Wednesday afternoon, waiting for our BSC meeting to start. The other club members were already there, but Kristy hadn't called the meeting to order yet, so I had a chance to look around the room at my new friends. It wasn't hard to remember my

10

first impressions of each of them. And I had to admit that, in every case, my first impressions did not tell the whole story.

Take Kristy Thomas, for example. She's the chairman of the BSC, and the first member I met, because she and I live in the same neighbourhood. First impression? Bossy. She definitely likes to be in charge. (I have to admit that we rubbed each other up the wrong way at first, because I also like running things.)

Now that I know Kristy a little better, I've come to realize that being bossy is one thing, but being a good leader is another. Kristy is definitely a good leader. She has excellent ideas, and she knows how to mobilize people to bring those ideas to life. A case in point: the BSC itself. Kristy and her friends had always done a lot of babysitting, but one day Kristy decided that parents would probably love to have just one phone number they could call to reach a whole group of reliable sitters, and she came up with the idea for the club.

The BSC worked wonderfully, right from the beginning. The club meets on Mondays, Wednesdays and Fridays from five-thirty till six. During those times, parents can—and do!—call to request sitters. We (the members of the club) split up the jobs as evenly as we can, and we each keep the money we make, except for a small amount we pay in subs each week. (That money covers what Kristy calls "administrative expenses", such as our phone bill, transportation costs and the occasional pizza.)

The club is very well organized, thanks to Kristy. She came up with the idea for the record book, in which the club secretary keeps track of client information and our schedules, and the club notebook, where we make notes about each job we take. These two tools make it easy for us to stay up-to-date with what's going on with the BSC's clients, and that makes our clients happy.

But the BSC isn't only about business. It's also about fun. That's where Kid-Kits come in. Kid-Kits (another of Kristy's brilliant ideas) are decorated boxes full of hand-me-down toys and games, as well as some new goodies. We each have one, and when we bring them to sitting jobs the kids go wild. All the BSC members love kids and enjoy their company, and vice versa.

Kristy is no exception to that rule. She adores kids, and it's a good thing, too, because there are a lot of them in her life. She coaches a kids' softball team, for one thing. Also, her family is huge. She has a younger brother, David Michael, plus two step-siblings (Karen and Andrew), whom

12

she acquired when her mother married Watson Brewer, who is a millionaire and also a really nice guy. (Kristy's dad is, as far as I can tell, totally out of the picture. He left the family when David Michael was just a baby.) Then there's Emily Michelle, the cutest toddler in the universe. She's Vietnamese, and Kristy's mum and Watson adopted her soon after they married.

Just to round out the picture of Kristy's full house, I'll tell you that Kristy's grandmother lives with the family, and that there are also two older Thomas boys, Charlie and Sam. They're at high school. Charlie owns a car, the appropriately named Junk Bucket, and he's the one who pockets those transportation costs we pay out of BSC subs. (He drives Kristy and me to our meetings.) The Thomas-Brewer clan also has a full menagerie of pets. I start wheezing and sneezing just thinking about them.

On to my next first impression: Kristy's best friend Mary Anne Spier, who is the BSC's secretary, which means she's in charge of the record book. When I first met her, she just seemed incredibly quiet and shy.

I think it's amazing that she and Kristy are best friends. They've known each other since babyhood, but they don't seem to have much in common apart from looks. Both of them are on the short side, with brown hair and brown eyes. Mary Anne cares a little more about how she dresses (Kristy doesn't care at all!), and has a trendier haircut. The cool clothes and hairstyle are apparently a fairly recent thing. For a long time Mary Anne's father (who brought her up on his own; her mum died when Mary Anne was just a baby) was very strict about how she dressed and behaved. He's remarried now, though, and it sounds as if Mary Anne's step-mother, Sharon, has been a good influence on him. Sharon has two children of her own from her first marriage; Jeff and Dawn. Both of them live in California with their father, although Dawn, who is thirteen, used to be in the BSC, and lived in Stoneybrook until recently. As well as being her stepsister, Dawn is Mary Anne's other best friend, and I think Mary Anne misses her *ferociously*.

Here's my deeper impression of Mary Anne: you couldn't have a better, more loyal, more sensitive friend. Kristy and Dawn are very lucky. So are Tigger and Logan, who are Mary Anne's grey kitten and her boyfriend. (I'm sure you can work out which is which.)

The BSC's vice-chairman is Claudia Kishi, who is Japanese-American and

14

really beautiful, with long, black hair and dark, almond-shaped eyes. She was elected unanimously to her position based on one thing: she has a phone in her room, with her own private line. That's why her room is BSC headquarters. We can make and take all the calls we like, without worrying about tying up anybody's family line.

I almost hate to tell you my first impression of Claudia, because I'm a little embarrassed by it now. The first time I met Claudia she was wearing the most outrageous outfit—some mixture of tie-dyed items, charity shop finds, and home-made jewellery. I don't remember the details. What I do remember is that she looked terrific . . . but a little weird. And I remember that she had just failed a simple little maths test. The fact is, I thought she was, well, a nutcase. But now that I know her better, I've discovered that she really isn't a nutcase at all. She's a creative, unique individual.

She's one of the most talented artists I've ever met, and everything she does, including the way she dresses, has a certain creative flair. That goes for maths tests, too, I suppose. And spelling. Claud is definitely a creative speller. Claudia's older sister Janine, who is an actual genius, is probably horrified by Claud's spelling. I quite like it, myself. It certainly makes reading the club notebook more interesting.

Claudia is also creative about hiding her two addictions—junk food and Nancy Drew books—from her parents, who disapprove of both. At first glance, Claudia's room seems like a Junk Food-and Mystery Novel-Free Zone. But if you were to open any cupboard or drawer and rummage around for a while, you'd probably find a bag of Doritos or a copy of *The Case of the Disappearing Diamonds*.

Claudia's best friend is Stacey McGill, who wears her blonde hair in a curly perm. She's the treasurer of the club, mostly because she's terrific at maths. Stacey grew up in New York City, so we have something in common, since Long Island is almost like an extension of the city. Her parents are divorced, and while Stacey chose to live with her mum in Stoneybrook, she visits her dad in Manhattan as often as she can.

First impression? I thought she was pretty and had great clothes, and that there wasn't a lot more to her. Was I wrong! There's much more to Stacey than meets the eye. She has a certain mature attitude. Partly, this is because she grew up in New York and is a little more sophisticated than most Stoneybrook kids, but it also has to do with the fact that Stacey has diabetes. Diabetes, in case you don't know, is a lifelong disease which prevents a person's body from processing sugars correctly. Stacey can never forget, even for one day, that she is diabetic. It's something she has to deal with all the time, by being ultra-careful with her diet, for example, and also by testing her blood sugar frequently and giving herself injections of insulin (which a healthy body produces and regulates naturally) every day.

Because of my asthma and allergies, I can relate to what Stacey has to deal with, and I admire and respect the way she copes. She's definitely more than just a pretty face.

OK, you've met the chairman, the V.C., the treasurer and the secretary of the BSC. I bet you're wondering what my role is in the club. Well, I'm the alternate officer, which means I step in for any other officer who can't get to a meeting. Dawn, Mary Anne's stepsister, was the alternate officer until she moved back to California for good. I've hardly met Dawn, but I have a strong impression of her: she's very mellow, very together and very health-conscious (she doesn't eat red meat). She has long blonde hair and blue eyes and she belongs to a West Coast babysitting club called the We ♥ Kids

Club. I'm looking forward to getting to know her better.

There are two junior members of the BSC, a pair of best friends called Jessi Ramsey and Mallory Pike. They're called junior members because they're eleven, while the rest of us are thirteen, and they're not allowed to sit at night except in their own homes.

My first impression of Jessi was that she had a one-track mind, that all she cared about was ballet. Now, it's true that Jessi is a dedicated—and talented—ballet student, and that dance is important to her, but she also has plenty of other interests. Jessi, who is African-American, is very close to her family: her parents, her baby brother Squirt, her younger sister Becca and her aunt Cecelia, who lives with the Ramseys. She and Mal both love horses, books (especially horse books!) and kids.

It's a good thing Mal loves kids, because she lives with seven of them. There are eight kids in her family, including a set of identical triplets! Mallory has curly reddish-brown hair and glasses and wears a brace (the clear kind). When I first met her I thought she was very serious. She wants to become an author and illustrator of children's books when she grows up, and she spends a lot of time writing and drawing. But Mal is full of fun, too, and we've had some great times sitting together for her siblings.

Finally, there are two associate members of the BSC: Shannon Kilbourne and Logan Bruno. They don't come to meetings regularly, but they help out whenever we're swamped with sitting jobs. Shannon lives in Kristy's and my neighbourhood, but she goes to a private school, so I haven't spent much time with her. She and Anna have become friends, partly because they both love music. My first impression of Shannon was that she was very studious, which she is. It turns out, though, that she's also very funny.

As for my first impression of Logan, who is Mary Anne's boyfriend, it was this: wow! He's cute. That's my second impression, too. He's an unusual guy in that he loves sports (he's a good athlete), but is also a world-class babysitter.

Neither Logan nor Shannon was at that Wednesday's meeting, and as a matter of fact I was barely there myself. I was so busy thinking about how much better I now knew each of the BSC members that I hardly noticed when Kristy called the meeting to order. I remember hearing the phone ring a few times, and I know some jobs were assigned. I munched absent-mindedly on some Pringles Claudia passed my way, but other than that I did not participate much in that day's meeting.

Until the end, that is. Just as Kristy began to adjourn the meeting, I remembered the job board. I couldn't believe I had almost forgotten about it. "Wait!" I cried. "I have something to tell you about."

"Where were you when I asked if there was any new business?" Kristy asked, frowning a little.

"On Mars, I think," I said, grinning at her. She lost the frown. "Anyway," I continued, "did you lot see that new jobs noticeboard at school? There's a posting on it that would be perfect for us. It's at the Greenbrook Club, and they're looking for all kinds of help, including child care. We could work there together. Wouldn't that be cool?"

"The Greenbrook Club?" asked Mary Anne. "Didn't that used to be called the Dark Woods Country Club?" She shook her head. "I don't know about working at that place. I seem to remember hearing some bad things about it."

"Like what?" I asked, confused. I had thought Greenbrook was a brand-new club. Now I was hearing things about a murky past.

"I'm not sure," admitted Mary Anne.

"I'll have to ask my dad and Sharon."

I felt a little let down, and my spirits dropped even further when Kristy said she was worried about our regular BSC clients being shortchanged if we all took on work at Greenbrook.

"That won't happen, I promise!" I said. "Look, why don't I just phone the place? I have the number right here." I pulled a slip of paper out of my pocket. "We don't have to commit ourselves to anything. We can just find out more about the work."

Claudia shrugged and passed me the phone. "Personally," she said, "I'd love the chance to do something new and different. There's been so little sitting lately, and I'm bored."

That was all I needed to hear. I dialled the number I'd copied down and spoke to a woman—I didn't quite catch her name—who invited the BSC members to visit Greenbrook the next day. My first impression of her? She sounded terrific, and straight away I knew that working at Greenbrook would be a sure cure for my February blues.

3rd CHAPTER

"I'm lucky Dad let me come," said Mary Anne, who was breathing hard as we ped- alled up a small hill.

"What could be so bad?" I asked. I was a little short of breath myself. "After all, Dark Woods closed twenty years ago. And the new owner is starting all over again."

It was Thursday afternoon, and we were on our way to Greenbrook, on bikes. It was a bit too chilly for a pleasant ride, but it still felt good to be outdoors. Kristy and I had walked home from school with the rest of the BSC friends, instead of taking the bus to our neighbourhood. Then Kristy had borrowed Dawn's bike, which is still stored in the big barn at Mary Anne's house, and Claudia had arranged for me to borrow Janine's. Mal and Jessi brought their bikes out of storage and joined us for a quick snack at Stacey's house, and then the BSC bike squad headed out.

As we rode along, Mary Anne filled us in on what her father and Sharon had said the night before, when she'd asked them about the job at Greenbrook. "They said there used to be all kinds of rumours about the Dark Woods Country Club, but they couldn't remember any of them specifically," she said. "Supposedly, it was incredibly exclusive. Only certain types of people were allowed to join. It just wasn't a very nice place. And then it suddenly closed, without any warning."

"Strange," Stacey commented.

"Yes, but my dad said he wasn't surprised. Something was wrong there."

"But now it's reopening, under new management," I pointed out, trying to sound optimistic.

"That *did* surprise him," said Mary Anne. "He couldn't imagine why anybody would want to be involved with that place, considering its history. I still don't know what happened there, but I do know it wasn't easy to talk him into letting me find out about this job."

"I'm with Abby," said Claudia. "What could be so bad about the place now that it has a new owner and everything?"

"Well, we may find out very soon," said Kristy, taking a hand off her handlebars to point towards a sign we were rapidly approaching. It said, in freshly painted white letters on a dark green background, GREENBROOK CLUB.

We turned into the winding drive and rode up to the imposing main building, which was built of stone and overlooked the open, rolling space of the golf course. There were tennis courts to the right of the building, and an outdoor pool (drained, for now) lay to the right of the courts. The area looked carefully land-scaped, with shrubs and trees and formal garden areas complete with fountains and benches.

"Wow!" breathed Jessi.

"Decent," Kristy said, sounding impressed in spite of herself.

"Looks like a cool place," I agreed. "Now, how do we find the owner? Maybe she knows." I nodded towards a blonde woman (who looked a little younger than my mum) walking towards us along one of the gravel paths. A boy of about seven was walking with her, holding her hand. Just as I was about to call to her, she surprised me by waving and smiling.

"You must be the girls from the club," she said as they approached us. "The BSC? Is that what you call yourselves?" The little boy looked up at us shyly. His sandy brown hair was cut short except for one longer tail down the back. His brown eyes had a slightly Asian look to them. He didn't look anything like the woman, and I wondered if they were related. I smiled at him.

"I'm Nicole Stanton-Cha," said the woman. "Everyone calls me Nikki. This is my son Stephen—he's seven. I'm the new owner of Greenbrook. Which of you did I speak to yesterday?"

I got off Janine's bike, put down the kick-stand, and, after taking off my bike helmet, shook her hand. "That was me," I said. "I'm Abby Stevenson. And these are my friends from the BSC." I introduced everyone, and they said hello to Nikki and Stephen. Claudia and Stacey were trying to fluff up their hair, which had been flattened by their helmets. Stephen smiled at everyone, but he stayed close by his mother's side.

Nikki seemed friendly and very matter-of-fact, and I liked her straight away. "Why don't we go into the main building for our interview?" she suggested.

We stowed our bikes near the side of the building and followed her inside. She led us down a hall (I caught a glimpse of a large, airy-looking dining room to the left) and into a cosy sitting room with library shelves and a fireplace. Nikki helped Stephen find a couple of books to look at and sent him into another room so we could attend to business.

Then Nikki asked us to tell her more about the BSC and how it operates, and Kristy jumped right in and gave her the whole story. I could tell that Nikki was impressed.

"Well, you girls certainly seem like responsible, hard-working kids, and that's exactly what I am looking for. We have all kinds of work available. For example, the decorator who's helping us redo the club needs an assistant. And we need people to do inventory, outdoor work and help with child care for visitors who come to tour the club. I hope a lot of people from town will do that." She smiled hopefully, and went on. "I'll arrange for a van to pick you and any other interested SMS students up after school and drive you here, and you're welcome to work any time you want. You'll need to keep track of your hours yourselves." She looked around at us. "Any questions?" she asked.

Mary Anne cleared her throat, but she looked too shy to speak. She gave Kristy a nudge. Kristy exchanged glances with her and nodded. "We heard some bad things about the old club here," she said. "Dark Woods?"

Nikki winced and shook her head. "Whatever you heard is probably true," she admitted. "Dark Woods was not a very nice place. It was discriminatory and elitist, which means," she added, apparently noticing our confused looks, "that they only let certain types of people join."

"Is that why it closed?" asked Stacey.

"Partly," said Nikki. "Some people sued, and as the club was already in debt, the legal bills were the last straw. The place was shut down just as it was, and all its possessions were frozen, in legal limbo, for years and years. Finally, some other investors and I bought the club, and we inherited everything. Fortunately, nothing was too run-down, because Mr Kawaja, the caretaker, stayed on. His wages were paid throughout the legal battle, and he took care of the buildings and grounds."

"So, with a little redecorating, it will be ready to open up again?" asked Jessi.

"Well, not exactly," answered Nikki. "I want to change as much as I can. I don't want Greenbrook to bear any resemblance to Dark Woods." She frowned. "I want Greenbrook to be open to anyone in the community, and I want the membership fees to be low. I want this to be a pleasant, open place where families can enjoy good times together." She paused, and I noticed a faraway look in her eyes, as if she were remembering something. "My family once belonged to Dark Woods," she said slowly. "And actually, I spent some of the happiest days of my life here."

"You used to live in Stoneybrook?" Mal asked.

Nikki nodded. "I grew up here," she said. "And I was here at the club all day, every day, every summer. I swam, I played tennis, I lay under the trees and read." She looked down at her hands, which were clenched in her lap. When she looked up again, her eyes were hard. "It wasn't until I was older that I realized what a sheltered world the club was, and how you had to come from a certain background to belong there. One day, when I was fourteen, I brought a new friend from school—her name was Rachel—to the club for a swim. We were having a terrific time, practising our swan dives, when suddenly, I noticed that all the club 'regulars' were giving me strange looks." Nikki raised her eyebrows. "Can you guess what was wrong?"

None of us said a word, but I had a feeling we were all thinking the same thing. Nikki didn't seem to notice that we hadn't answered. Absorbed in her story, she went on.

"At last one of my father's friends pulled me aside and told me it wasn't appropriate to bring 'such a guest' to the club. I was confused, because I'd brought other friends there before. Then I realized that Rachel was Jewish.''

I drew in a sharp breath. My family is Jewish, too. That means I wouldn't have been welcome at Dark Woods, either. Suddenly, I felt sick. "That's awful!" I cried.

Nikki nodded. "I thought so, too. I vowed never to return to the club. And I didn't. I left Stoneybrook when I finished school, and I didn't come back until I learned that the club was up for sale. Now Stephen and my husband and I are eager to make a life here.''

"Your parents must be thrilled to have you back," I said, without thinking. (I do that a lot.)

Nikki shook her head, looking sad. "My mother passed away five years ago. And I haven't talked to my father for almost ten years. He does still live in Stoneybrook, but he wants nothing to do with me. The day I told him I was marrying a Korean man was the day he stopped speaking to me.'' Nikki held her chin up, but I could see that she was very upset. "He won't see his grandchild, either.''

A Korean man. That explained Stephen's looks. How could Nikki's father be so awful?

29

"Has—has your father ever met your husband?" asked Mary Anne softly.

"No," replied Nikki. "And the funny thing is, I'm sure they'd like each other. Thomas is an excellent businessman. He's in Korea on business right now, in fact. I know my father would admire him."

"Maybe one day—" Mary Anne began.

Nikki shook her head. "No, it's too late. It's been this way for so long now that I'm used to it. Anyway," she said, jumping up and brushing together her hands, as if she were trying to rid them of dirt, "I think it's time for me to get back to work. I've enjoyed our interview, and I hope to see you all here soon." She spoke brightly, but her eyes still looked troubled.

"If you ever need a babysitter for Stephen, please phone us," said Kristy. "He seems like a nice kid."

Nikki smiled gratefully. "He is," she said. "And I might—phone you, that is. I'm sure I will need a sitter for Stephen, as I'll be spending every day here. Soon he'll be bored wandering around Greenbrook all afternoon while I work."

Kristy gave her the BSC phone number, and asked where she and her family lived. They had just moved into Mallory's neighbourhood.

A few minutes later, Nikki and Stephen waved to us as we rode off down the long

30

drive. We waved back. It looked as though the BSC and the Greenbrook Club were going to be a good match.

4th CHAPTER

Cokie Mason folded her arms. She looked peeved. "I don't see what's so strange about it," she said. "Why do you think it's strange?" She sounded more angry than curious.

"Oooh, Cokie's angry," teased Alan Gray, who was sitting in the seat behind her. He grinned at Kristy. "What *is* so strange?" he asked. "Go ahead, Kristy. Let's see you find your way out of this one."

Kristy shot Alan a nasty look, and he grabbed the guy sitting next to him. "Protect me, Cary," he cried in a high voice.

Typical back-of-the-bus behaviour. I glanced at Rick Chow and Stacey, who were sharing the seat opposite where Kristy and I were sitting. Stacey rolled her eyes at me. It was Monday afternoon, and we were on our way to Greenbrook for

32

our first day of work. (We'd be finished in time for our BSC meeting.) I'd been looking forward to it, but I'd forgotten one thing: the job was open to all SMS students, which meant I wouldn't be able to choose my co-workers. Or my co-commuters. If I had been able to choose, you can bet I wouldn't have been sitting on a bus with Alan, Cokie and Cary.

Alan is, as Kristy often points out, "the most immature boy in eighth grade". She's known him for years, and judging from her stories, he still acts exactly the way he did when they were in fifth grade. I can see for myself that he still makes stupid jokes and thinks the best way to let a girl know you like her is to punch her on the arm.

As for Cary Retlin, nobody at SMS has known him long. Like me, he moved here recently. But remember what I said about first impressions being lasting? Well, Cary's made quite a first impression at SMS, as a practical joker and a mischief-maker, mostly. He's kind of a puzzle, and nobody in the BSC has had much luck working out what makes him tick. Mary Anne and Logan are both especially curious about him, as they suspect he was the one responsible for some disruptive notes the two of them received not long ago: notes to Mary Anne in what looked like

Logan's handwriting (but wasn't), and vice versa. They were never able to confirm their suspicions, and as the notes eventually stopped, they let it drop.

What about Cokie? Again, I don't know her very well, as I'm new here, but I can say one thing for sure: she and I will never be best buddies. Cokie is always looking out for Number One, if you know what I mean. Her overall attitude is, "What's in it for me?" She's done a lot of nasty things to members of the BSC, but the nastiest of all, and the one that nobody will ever forgive, was when she tried to steal Logan away from Mary Anne. How could she?

Just thinking about it made me furious. I glared at Cokie, who was glaring at Kristy, who was glaring at Alan, who was still pretending to hide behind Cary. Rick, who is one of the nicer guys at SMS, just ignored the whole scene.

Kristy had asked Cokie why she was interested in working at Greenbrook. "It seems strange that you'd want to go there," she'd said.

That was when Cokie started acting offended and insisting that it wasn't strange at all.

"I didn't mean to offend you," said Kristy (lying through her teeth). "It's just that renovating a club seems like such dirty work. Not your style."

34

Cokie sniffed. "Well, you're right," she said. "Normally I wouldn't be interested. But I'm doing it so I'll have an 'in' at the club. They're going to need hostesses— beautiful ones—when it opens."

Alan snorted. "You?" he asked. "You're not—" Just then he caught the full force of Cokie's glare, and he saved himself. "You're not, er, *old* enough to be a hostess, are you?"

Cokie shrugged, rummaged in her bag, and pulled out a pot of lip gloss. "I suppose I'll find out," she said. She unscrewed the top of the pot, dipped her little finger into it, and started to smooth shiny pink gloss on to her lips.

"What about you?" asked Alan, turning to Cary. "Why are you going to work at Greenbrook?"

"I need the money," Cary said seriously. Then (I think I was the only one who noticed this, because he quickly ducked down, pretending to check his rucksack) he blushed and looked very embarrassed. A nanosecond later he had changed the subject, and soon he and Alan were joking about this English teacher, Mr Fiske, who has vile taste in ties.

Soon the bus driver drove past the Greenbrook sign and followed the long drive to the main building. When the bus stopped, we all piled out.

35

"Hey, there!" called Nikki, emerging from the main building with Stephen in tow. Two women and a man followed her out of the door. One of the women had flaming red hair in a mass of curls around her head. The other had straight, platinum blonde hair cut in a precise bob. The man, who looked Asian, was small and wiry and wore a black smock with many pockets.

"I'm so glad you're all here," said Nikki, smiling. "Let's see if I remember everybody's names." She pointed to each of us in turn. "Cary, Alan, Kristy, Stacey, Abby, Rick and Marguerite. How's that?"

Everybody nodded and smiled, except for Kristy, who was too busy staring at Cokie to answer. "Marguerite?" she asked, raising her eyebrows.

"You know that's my real name," said Cokie defensively, turning to face Kristy. Then she lowered her voice. "It makes me sound older, don't you think?"

Kristy just smirked. Cokie, looking defeated, turned back to Nikki. "You can call me Cokie," she mumbled.

"Fine," said Nikki. "Welcome, everyone."

Kristy stepped forward. "I just wanted to let you know that not everyone in the BSC will be here every day," she said. "Some members will turn up every day, but we have to keep on top of our business, too."

"I understand," Nikki replied. "All of you are welcome any time, and you can work as many or as few hours as you want. I'll leave signing-in sheets at the reception desk inside. Now, I'd like to introduce some of the Greenbrook team. This," she said, putting her hand on the man's shoulder, "is Mr Kawaja. None of us would be here now if it weren't for him. He's responsible for keeping this club from turning into a jungle."

Mr Kawaja nodded briefly, but did not smile or speak.

"And this is Darcy, our decorator," continued Nikki, indicating the blonde woman, "and Miss Cureton, our architect." They smiled at us. "As far as work today goes," said Nikki, "I have several different jobs available." She consulted the clipboard she'd been carrying. "First, I'll need someone to help Stephen with his reading homework while I go over some bills."

"I'll do that," volunteered Stacey, smiling at Stephen. He gave her a tiny, shy smile in return.

"Great," said Nikki. "Second, Mr Kawaja is looking for helpers to work on tidying up the grounds. The first task will be to start at the maintenance shed and pick up all the sticks and twigs that have fallen over the winter. We'll put them in a pile and have a bonfire one night soon. Is that your plan, Mr Kawaja?" She turned to him, smiling. He nodded, and I thought I saw one corner of his mouth twitch slightly, but I really couldn't say that he smiled back.

"I'll help with that," I said quickly. I wanted to be outside. It wasn't too cold, and while the sky wasn't exactly blue, I could see the sun peeling through the clouds once in a while.

"Me, too," said Cary.

Ugh!

"I can pick up sticks," volunteered Alan, flexing his biceps like a body builder.

Double ugh! Oh well, I didn't have to stay with them. We could cover different parts of the grounds. I was still happy to have an outdoor assignment.

"I need someone to follow me around and take down notes for me as I look over the buildings," said Miss Cureton.

"I'd love to do that," said Kristy. "I've always wondered what an architect does."

"I'll come!" said Rick at the same time.

"I'll take both of you," Miss Cureton said.

"And I desperately need someone to assist me," said Darcy. "We'll be reupholstering all that hideous furniture in the lounge, and we need new carpeting as well. I need someone to hold up the fabric swatches so I can make a decision."

"Swatches?" Cokie spoke up. "I love swatches! I'll help you, Miss——"

"It's just Darcy," said the woman. "You know, like Madonna or Cher."

"Darcy," repeated Cokie, sounding impressed. Behind her back, Alan and Cary mimicked her starstruck look, letting their eyes cross and their mouths hang open. Luckily, nobody but me seemed to notice.

"We're ready, then," said Nikki. "Have fun, everybody."

"But don't go into the maze," Stephen said suddenly. He hadn't said a word before that. He'd just been standing close to and slightly behind his mother, watching as we split into teams.

"The maze?" I asked. "What's that?"

"Oh—oh, it's nothing," said Nikki. "It's just that there's this garden maze in the grounds. You know, one of those old-fashioned mazes made out of high hedges. We'd rather you didn't enter it."

"Why, will we be lost for ever if we do?" cracked Alan.

Nikki didn't smile, and I noticed that Mr Kawaja looked more serious than ever. "Just avoid it, if you would," Nikki said firmly. Then she stood up a little straighter. "All right, then? Let's start working!"

We split up and set off in different directions. Nikki, Stacey and Stephen went into the main building, with Cokie and Darcy following them. Rick, Kristy and Miss Cureton went off towards a small pagoda-like building near the tennis courts. And Alan, Cary, Mr Kawaja and I set out for the maintenance shed, which was tucked behind the main building. It was filled with rakes, shovels and all kinds of smaller gardening tools, as well as bags of peat moss and fertilizer. A motorized lawn mower and a small tractor were parked in the middle of the shed.

Alan hopped on to the tractor seat and made motor noises. "Vroom, vroom!" he said. He looked around, grinning, waiting for us to laugh. I rolled my eyes. Cary shook his head. And Mr Kawaja frowned and made a hand signal that said, unmistakably, "Get off the tractor. Now."

Alan climbed off.

Then Mr Kawaja handed us each a pair of gardening gloves and took us outside to show us a row of wheelbarrows lined up against the shed wall. Then he looked at me expectantly. (I wondered if he were physically unable to speak.)

I realized he wasn't going to tell us anything further. "I'll go that way," I said, waving towards the tennis courts and taking one of the wheelbarrows.

Mr Kawaja nodded.

Alan and Cary each grabbed a wheelbarrow, too, and took off in different directions. For me, at least, the rest of the day at Greenbrook was great. I worked on my own, feeling my muscles stretched as I stooped to pick up branches, then threw them into the wheelbarrow. I covered a good amount of territory, from the tennis courts to one of the formal gardens.

Only two things about the afternoon seemed weird. First of all, I kept seeing this big white limousine cruising around the club, circling on the roads that connect the main building and the other buildings on the grounds. The windows of the limo were tinted, so there was no way I could see inside. I wondered who was riding in it, and why they were circling like a great white shark.

The other weird thing happened when I ran into Mr Kawaja near the formal garden. I was walking along a hedge, picking up small evergreen branches, when suddenly he appeared in front of me, glaring at me and shaking his head. I was surprised, until I realized that the hedge must be part of the maze Stephen and Nikki had mentioned. Once I worked that

41

out, I was dying to look into its entrance (wouldn't *you* be curious?), but Mr Kawaja crossed his arms and stood directly in my path, so I had no choice but to turn and walk away.

Apart from that, our first day at Greenbrook was a success. True, something seemed a little "off" about the place, but hey, a job's a job. It wasn't as if there were anything sinister about what I'd seen. I wasn't going to let my imagination run away with me. I was just going to work hard and try to make it through February.

5th CHAPTER

Tuesday

Mystery Alert!! Time to pull out the mystery notebook and start keeping track. I knew there was something fishy about that place! There's more going on than meets the eye at Greenbrook. It has to do with the club's shadowy history — but we wouldn't know anything about it if we hadn't run into one of the BSC's favourite fellow detectives....

Tuesday was my second day of work at Greenbrook. I'd been looking forward to it all morning. Claudia and Mary Anne made up the rest of the BSC crew that afternoon, and while Cary and Cokie were both there too, Alan and Rick were not.

Once again, Nikki met the bus and helped assign jobs. Cokie ran off with Darcy (both of them talking excitedly about "paisley damask window treatments"), and Claudia volunteered to work with Miss Cureton. Cary, Mary Anne and I followed Mr Kawaja to the maintenance shed, where, without saying a word, he handed out pruning shears to each of us. Then he led us into the garden and showed us how to shape and prune the shrubs.

Mary Anne and I started working on opposite sides of a giant bush. It looked dead to me: all I could see was a tangle of bare brown twigs. But when I said so, Mr Kawaja pointed out small swellings on the tips of the branches, and I realized that they were the beginnings of buds. I worked carefully after that; suddenly it was easy to imagine how the bush would look in the summer, covered with green leaves. Mary Anne and I snipped away, piling the twigs we cut off into a wheelbarrow parked on the garden path that meandered past our bush.

44

The day was, as the weatherman had promised, partly sunny. I've never completely understood the difference between "partly cloudy" and "partly sunny", but in this case "partly sunny" meant that the sun spent more time warming the top of my head then it did hiding behind the clouds. It wasn't too cold out; I was wearing a fleece jacket over a woollen shirt, and I was perfectly warm, except for a refreshing tingling around my nose and ears. I felt so glad to be outside, doing something, that I started to sing while I pruned.

In case you're wondering, Anna is the twin who received all the musical genes. I sing like a frog.

But Mary Anne didn't seem to mind. In fact, she grinned at me through the branches and joined right in. I led us through every song I remembered from my mum's "girl groups" tape, starting with "Leader of the Pack" and running through "Dancing in the Street", "Please Mr Postman" and "My Boyfriend's Back". I *adore* all those old girl-group hits.

Finally, we sang this Supremes song called "Stop! In the Name of Love". I couldn't help myself. I put down my pruners and started adding choreography, Motown style. Hand gestures, spins, the whole bit. Mary Anne followed along, belting out the lyrics—something she never would have done if we hadn't been in the middle of a deserted garden.

"Stop in the name of love," I crooned, holding out a hand in front of me like a traffic cop.

"Before you break my heart," sang Mary Anne, pointing first at me, then at herself, then tracing a heart in the air.

We yodelled the next line at the top of our lungs.

Then we repeated the line, a little softer. Just softly enough, in fact, so that we could hear another voice joining ours for the chorus. Mary Anne and I stopped singing and exchanged surprised looks. Then she clapped a hand over her mouth, and her eyes grew round as she looked past me, over my shoulder to the path where the wheelbarrow was standing. I turned around just in time to see a tall, black-haired man break into loud laughter.

"Which one of you is Diana Ross?" he asked, smiling.

"Sergeant Johnson!" Mary Anne cried, blushing a deep, deep red. "What are *you* doing here?"

"Enjoying the show, at the moment," he said, still grinning. He nodded to me. "Aren't you Abby?" he asked.

"I am," I answered. "And I think I owe

you a big thank you, for saving my life at Shadow Lake."

Sergeant Johnson waved a hand at me. "It was nothing," he said. "All in the line of duty."

Maybe I should stop here and explain who Sergeant Johnson is and why he knows the members of the BSC. First of all, you should know that the BSC members have been involved in more than one Stoneybrook mystery. (That's why we have a mystery notebook, in which we keep track of clues and suspects and such.) We've been mixed up with all kinds of nasty criminals, a fact I didn't know when I agreed to go on what was supposed to be a fun skiing holiday at Shadow Lake recently. It turned into the scariest weekend of my life. Sergeant Johnson helped to save the day by taking a tip from Mary Anne seriously and making a timely phonecall to the Shadow Lake police.

The other members of the BSC got to know Sergeant Johnson the first time they helped the Stoneybrook Police solve a mystery. Ever since then, he's been on our side. He's always been receptive to club members who've offered him suspicions, clues or possible evidence.

"Are you girls working for Mrs Stanton-Cha?" Sergeant Johnson asked.

We nodded. "How about you?" I

asked. He hadn't given Mary Anne a straight answer when she'd asked why he was there, and I was curious.

"Actually, I'm here on police business," he said. Then he paused. "Or maybe it's personal business," he continued, scratching his head, "as I'm not on duty right now. I'm here in my own time."

"Do you often do police work in your own time?" I asked. Mary Anne nudged me, and I knew she thought I was asking too many questions. But I was interested.

"Not often," he replied, shaking his head. "This case is different, though. According to the department, it's closed. But I don't see it that way. This case is very close to my heart, and it won't be closed for me until . . . until. . . Well, let me see where to begin." Sergeant Johnson gestured towards a bench.

"When I was a kid, my best friend was David Follman," he began, as soon as we were settled on the bench. "When we grew up, I became a policeman and he became a reporter. Thirty years ago, he began an investigation into some dirty doings at Dark Woods."

"Like how creepy they were about not letting certain people join?" I asked.

"Worse than that. David had heard rumours about a secret society operating

48

out of the club, a group of men who were involved in a blackmail and extortion ring. They were powerful, made more powerful by banding together. They acted illegally to force the local townspeople and merchants to do what they wanted them to do: to vote a certain way, for example, or to use a certain contractor to build their new school."

"That's awful!" cried Mary Anne.

"David thought so, too," said Sergeant Johnson. "He went undercover to try to infiltrate the society. And I think he was succeeding. But before he could publish his findings, or even share them with me, David died."

"Oh!" Mary Anne gasped. I felt a knot start to grow in my stomach. I hate to hear about people dying suddenly, because it makes me think of my dad.

"How did he die?" I asked.

"In a car accident," Sergeant Johnson answered, and my knot grew tighter. "A mysterious car accident. Nobody was ever able to work out why his car went off the road where it did, up near an embankment on Route Five. There were no skid marks, and nothing was wrong with his car's steering. But David died instantly when the car rolled down the hill."

"And you think he was murdered," I said slowly. This was heavy stuff.

"I do," said Sergeant Johnson. "But I've never been able to prove it. Everybody in the force thinks I'm crazy to keep the case alive, but I just haven't been able to let it go. And now that this club has reopened, I think I'll do some real investigating."

"Do you have any clues at all?" asked Mary Anne, leaning forward with a gleam in her eye. I could see that she was already hooked by this mystery. I was, too.

"Only one," Sergeant Johnson answered, "and I've never been able to make sense of it. The last thing David ever said to me was 'Watch where you step.' I've always been convinced that somehow this was a riddle, a clue I should have been able to work out. But I have no idea what it means." He shook his head.

The three of us sat silently for a moment. Then, suddenly, I heard footsteps on the path, and Mr Kawaja appeared, pushing a wheelbarrow full of twigs and sticks. Cary, who was walking next to him, caught my eye and nodded. I thought I saw him wink, but I wasn't sure. Had he and Mr Kawaja heard any of what Sergeant Johnson had just told us? I hoped not, although I couldn't work out why it would matter. I suppose I was just excited about this mystery Mary Anne and I had stumbled on to, and I wanted to keep it ours alone.

Except for sharing it with the rest of the BSC members, of course. We told Claudia about it during the journey home, and she was fascinated. Mary Anne invited us to dinner at her house, so we could talk it over some more. Claudia had a sitting job and couldn't come, but I accepted. It turned out that Sharon, Mary Anne's stepmother, had invited other guests, too: her parents, Dawn's Granny and Pop-Pop (that's what everyone calls them), who have lived in Stoneybrook all their lives.

Naturally, Mary Anne and I jumped at the opportunity to grill them about Dark Woods. At first, they didn't want to talk about it, but we barraged them with questions, and eventually they told us a few interesting facts. Such as, the mayor when Dark Woods closed was called Armstrong, and he was unpopular, except among the people in his favour. He was known (as Pop-Pop put it) as "a strongarmer", which meant that he had ways of making people do what he wanted them to do. Pop-Pop also mentioned that he'd heard rumours about the secret society, and that he suspected that Armstrong might have been part of it, along with— guess who?—Mr Stanton, Nikki's father!

Granny laughed when Mr Stanton's name came up, and called him "Mayor Armstrong's right-hand fool". She didn't seem to have much respect for him. And she was surprised to hear that he was still living in the Stoneybrook area. As far as she knew, she said, he had moved away a long time ago. And as for Armstrong, she told us that he must be very old, or even dead, by now. She remembered hearing that he had stayed in Stoneybrook all through World War II because of a heart problem. "All the other men went off to war, except him," she said.

Very interesting. I couldn't wait to write the day up in the mystery notebook. I also couldn't wait to return to Greenbrook. This job was turning out to be much more than just a February distraction!

6th CHAPTER

Wednesday

Stephen is a nice kid. Now, all we have to do is convince the other kids to believe it. Or rather, we have to convince Stephen to believe it. At least I am starting to understand why he's so shy. . . .

Mal had the first official BSC job with
Stephen. By "official", I mean that she
wasn't just helping him with his homework over at Greenbrook while his mum
and the other BSC members worked, the
way Stacey had on our first day there.
This time, Nikki had phoned during
Monday's meeting to arrange a sitting job.
Mal, who had taken the job, went over to
the Stanton-Chas' house on Wednesday
afternoon. She talked for a bit to Nikki,
who then left for Greenbrook. (Nikki had
already been at Greenbrook most of the
day, but had returned home just long
enough to greet Stephen after school and
spend half an hour with him.)

Stephen had hung back, sitting on the
stairs while Mal and Nikki chatted in the
front hall. Mal thought he had a right to
feel shy, as they'd met for only a few
minutes during Mal's first day at
Greenbrook. After Nikki left, Mal sat next
to him on the stairs. "Do you like your
new house?" she asked.

"It's OK," he answered, barely glancing at her.

"I like it a lot," said Mal, looking
around. "It feels very homey."

Stephen didn't say anything.

"I bet you're going to have lots of new
friends here," said Mal. "Stoneybrook
Elementary is a great school, and there

are tons of kids in this neighbourhood."

Stephen looked down at his shoes and
muttered something.

"What did you say?" asked Mal.

Stephen muttered a little louder. "I
don't have any friends." He looked so sad
and lonely that Mal's heart broke just a
little.

"Well, not yet, you don't," she said,
trying to sound cheerful. "After all, you've
just moved here. You're new in school,
and you're new in the neighbourhood.
But it won't take you long to make friends,
believe me."

Stephen looked doubtful.

"Tell you what," said Mal, smacking
her knees and standing up. "How about
if we go out for a walk? It's not a bad day
out there, and I bet a lot of kids are playing
outside. I know just about everybody in
this neighbourhood, and I can introduce
you. How does that sound?"

"OK," agreed Stephen. He went to the
cupboard and found his jacket and a baseball cap. "I'm ready," he said as soon as
he'd put on the cap and zipped up his
jacket. He looked less sad and more hopeful, Mal thought.

"Great!" said Mal. "Let's go." She left
a note, in case Nikki came home early
(BSC members always try to do that), and

she and Stephen went out of the door and down the street.

The first kid they saw was four-year-old Brian Williams, whom Mal knew slightly, who was playing with toy cars in his front garden while his mother sat on the porch steps with his baby brother. Mal waved to Mrs Williams and called hello to Brian. "Mallory Pike!" Brian cried, running to give Mal a hug. Mal knew Brian was too young to be a real friend to Stephen, but she decided to introduce them anyway.

Brian stared at Stephen for a moment. He said hi, and Stephen said hi in return. But then Brian turned his attention back to Mallory. "When are you going to baby-sit for me again, Mallory Pike?" he asked. "I want to hear the rest of that story we were making up, the one about the bunny."

Mal smiled and promised Brian she'd see him soon. Then she and Stephen went down the street again. "He's a nice boy," said Mal.

"He's a little kid," grumbled Stephen. "And he didn't even like me, anyway."

Mal glanced at Stephen, and noticed that his mouth was turned down and that he had that sad and lonely look again. "He'd like you if he knew you better," said Mal. "Maybe one day while I'm sitting for him—"

"Do you know any older kids?" interrupted Stephen.

"I certainly do," said Mal. She looked up the street. "In fact, there are three of them, right now!" She pointed to the Braddocks' house. There, in the side garden, were three girls: Haley Braddock and Vanessa, Mal's sister, who are both nine, and Charlotte Johanssen, who is eight. The three of them are kids the BSC sits for regularly.

"Hey, you lot!" said Mal. "What are you doing?"

"We're practising cheers," answered Haley. "Softball season is right around the corner, you know."

"How does this sound?" asked Vanessa, striking a pose. "Krushers, Krushers, you're the ones! You make softball so much fun!" (Vanessa wants to be a poet, and she rhymes all the time—not just when she's cheering.) She bounced around energetically as she yelled, pretending to shake a pair of pom-poms. Haley and Charlotte bounced and yelled along with her. As you might have guessed, they are cheerleaders for Kristy's Krushers, which is the name of the team Kristy coaches.

"Sounds terrific," said Mal. "Hey, I have somebody I want you to meet. This is Stephen Stanton-Cha, and he's just

57

moved into the neighbourhood. His parents are the new owners of the country club."

"Cool," said Haley, smiling at Stephen. "My dad's going to play golf there." She peered at Stephen, interested. "How come you have two last names?"

Stephen frowned, and didn't say a word. Mal sensed that he was hanging back again. "Stanton is his mum's name, and Cha is his dad's," she explained. "Stephen's mother has been working very hard making sure the club will be ready by golf season," she told Haley.

"I can't wait! Greenbrook sounds great," rhymed Vanessa.

"Vanessa is my sister," Mal explained. "I've told her all about Greenbrook."

"Oh," Stephen said. He hardly looked at Vanessa.

"My mum's going to join, too," Charlotte piped up. "She plays tennis a lot in the summer."

Stephen nodded, but didn't seem very interested. Mal wished he weren't so shy. Maybe if he were more outgoing he'd have an easier time making friends.

"Well, we have to keep practising," said Haley. "You lot can stay and watch if you want." Again, she smiled at Stephen, but Stephen didn't respond.

58

"I think we'll keep walking," said Mal. "See you around!"

She led Stephen down the street, unsure if she should comment on his behaviour. She didn't want to make him feel self-conscious about it, but he certainly wouldn't make friends quickly, unless he overcame his shyness. Before she could decide what to say, she spotted her youngest sisters, Claire and Margo, who were in the Pikes' garden playing a game they call Little Mermaid and Friends. It's a mish-mash of their favourite films (lately they've been introducing Ariel and Pocahontas to Simba, the Lion King), but they love it, and it keeps them busy for hours.

"Hi, Claire," said Mal. "Hi, Margo. Listen, this is Stephen. I wanted him to meet you—and everybody else. Where *is* everybody?" Normally, a lot more kids would have been in the Pikes' garden.

Claire shrugged. "I don't know, Mallory-silly-goo-goo!" She's five, and loves talking nonsense. She peered at Stephen. "Are you Chinese?" she asked. Stephen shook his head, frowning.

"They're all over at the Arnolds," said Margo, who didn't seem to notice the way Stephen was glowering at Claire. "Hi, Stephen." Margo is seven, just Stephen's age. "Aren't you in Mr Anderson's class? I think I've seen you at school."

Stephen nodded. He'd lost the angry look and now he just looked shy.

Margo waited for him to say something, but he didn't. "Want to play with us? You could be Aladdin," she offered. "Or you could be Simba."

"How come he gets to be Simba?" whined Claire. "I *never* get to be Simba."

"That's OK," Stephen said hastily. "You can be Simba. I don't know how, anyway." He backed away a little, looking as if he wanted to be anywhere else but in the Pikes' front garden. "Let's go home," he said to Mal. "I have some reading homework to do, I think."

"Let's just drop in on the Arnolds," said Mal. "I want you to meet the rest of my brothers and sisters." Stephen looked reluctant, but Mal smiled persuasively and at last he nodded. As they walked across the street, Mal pointed out that her sister had invited him to play.

"Only because they have too many parts and only two people to play them," said Stephen. "She didn't really like me."

Mal raised her eyebrows, but she decided to try one last time.

Mal could hear loud voices coming from the Arnolds' back garden, so she led

Stephen around the house to find out who was there. "Yess!" she said to herself as she rounded the corner and saw a garden full of kids. There were Marilyn and Carolyn Arnold, who are eight-year-old identical twins; Jake Kuhn, who's also eight; Matt Braddock (Haley's brother), who's seven; plus four Pike kids: Adam, Jordan and Byron, who are ten (they're the identical triplets); and Nicky, who's eight.

"Hey, everyone!" called Mal. "You look busy. What are you up to?"

The kids ran to her and surrounded her and Stephen, all talking at the same time.

"We're going to have a club!" exclaimed Byron and Adam together.

"We're making a miniature golf course," added Jordan.

"It's a kids' club!" said Nicky, who was staring curiously at Stephen.

"Like the country club, only for us kids," explained Jake.

Matt held up a golf club—a putter—and grinned. He's deaf, and communicates mostly with sign language.

"What a terrific idea," said Mal. "A neighbourhood club! I bet Stephen would like to help." She introduced him to everyone and explained who he was, thinking they'd love to have the son of a real country-club owner helping them.

Everyone smiled at Stephen and said hello, but once again, he hung back shyly. Before long, the kids had begun working, gathering materials and supplies for their golf course.

After a few minutes, Mal gave up and walked Stephen back to his home. She talked to him gently about how he needed to *be* friendly in order to make friends, and asked if he could tell her why he was so shy.

"I just don't fit in anywhere," said Stephen finally, looking down at the sidewalk. "I'm not white, I'm not Korean, and I'm certainly not Chinese! I'm just nothing. I'm not like those other kids. Don't you see how they stare at me, and ask about my name? I'm different. At school the other day, a kid said to me, 'What are you, anyway?' I hate it when they ask me that!"

Mal felt awful for Stephen. She knew it couldn't be easy being the new kid at school. He must be lonely, and he must miss his dad, who was going to be away for so long on business. And on top of that, feeling different because he was bi-racial must be painful. "That must hurt your feelings," she said. "But you know what? I happen to think it's really cool that you are both Korean and American. You're lucky to have such a special

62

heritage." Mal's words seemed to help a little. But Mal knew it might take some time for Stephen to appreciate his background. She also knew that she and the rest of the BSC members could help Stephen through the tough time he was having, if only he'd let us.

7th CHAPTER

Over the next few days, none of us spent much time with Stephen. We were working hard at the club every day after school, and working hard on the mystery of Dark Woods, too. The mystery notebook made the rounds, and everybody had something to add: a clue, a mysterious event, suspicious circumstances.

That limo was really creeping me out.

Me, too. At least now we know who it is.

Yes, but that still doesn't explain what he's doing here.

Very suspicious, I agree.

That was Mary Anne and Stacey's mystery notebook entry from the day they

64

were at Greenbrook, raking the pebbled drives that circle the grounds of the club. At first the day seemed like any other. Groups of prospective members were touring the club while Mr Kawaja and the other workers rushed around busily. Then Mary Anne and Stacey noticed that same white limo cruising around, the one I'd seen on our first day at Greenbrook. They kept a nervous watch on it. The driver didn't seem to follow a pattern, Stacey told me. It was as if he were driving aimlessly.

That is, until the limo came to a stop near the tennis courts, and an elderly man climbed out of the back. Mary Anne and Stacey pretended to continue raking, but they were watching the man closely. He walked from the car to a bench, sat down, and stared into the distance.

"What's he looking at?" asked Stacey, straining to see.

"I can't tell," Mary Anne answered.

"Let's sneak up closer," suggested Stacey. Mary Anne looked at her as if she were crazy; but then shrugged and followed as Stacey, still pretending to rake, moved closer and closer to the figure on the bench. Being closer didn't help them work out who the man was—they still didn't recognize him—but it *did* give them an idea of what he might be looking at.

By standing directly behind him and following his gaze, they saw that he was watching someone bounce a tennis ball off the backboard in one of the tennis courts. And that someone was Stephen Stanton-Cha, who was hanging around at Greenbrook for a few hours that afternoon.

Stacey and Mary Anne exchanged looks behind the man's back. Then they moved off, still raking, until they were out of his hearing range. "This is really creepy," said Mary Anne.

"I don't like it either," agreed Stacey. "I think we should tell Nikki. Let's go and find her right now."

They ran into the main building. "I'll check the office," said Stacey. "You look in the dining room."

Mary Anne nodded and set off down the main hallway. But she hadn't gone three steps before something stopped her in her tracks. "Stacey," she called. "Wait! Come back! Look at this!"

Stacey joined her where she stood, near a display of photographs of former Dark Woods members. "What is it? I can't believe Darcy hasn't taken these old things down yet," she said.

"Good thing she hasn't," said Mary Anne, pointing to one of the pictures. "Otherwise, we might not have been able to identify that man we just saw watching Stephen."

Stacey glanced at the picture. "Oh, wow!" she whispered, when she saw the caption. It read *Paul R. Stanton*, and the picture above it showed, without a doubt, a younger version of the man they'd just been spying on.

"Stephen's grandfather!" said Mary Anne. "It must be."

"How strange," said Stacey. Then they moved off, first to find Nikki, who was surprised to hear that her father had been on the premises, and then to search for the rest of the BSC members, to tell us to keep an eye out for the white limo and Mr Stanton.

Watch where you step. Watch where you step. That phrase has been going around and around in my head. And finally, I think I may have figured out what David Follman meant by it

Kristy was obsessed with trying to work out what Sergeant Johnson's reporter friend had meant by his last warning. First, she—and other BSC members she recruited—toured the entire club, examining every step and staircase in the grounds. She didn't find any hidden secrets, although she did make a mental note to tell Darcy that some of the woodwork was in need of touching up.

Next, Kristy rearranged the letters in WATCH WHERE YOU STEP, as if it were an anagram, but didn't come up with anything more meaningful than CHEW HER WAY OUT PETS. That didn't make any sense at all.

At last, Kristy stumbled across a clue—literally! She was walking through the dining room when she tripped and almost fell. She had put down a hand to catch herself, and now she noticed that a corner of the old, stained, brown carpet wasn't completely tacked down.

"No wonder I nearly fell," she muttered to herself. Then, just out of curiosity, she flipped up the carpet to see what kind of flooring lay underneath. It turned out to be wooden planks, but that wasn't what made her draw a sudden breath. It was the stain she saw, across the corner of the flooring. A distinct, deep purplish-red stain that looked a little like writing. Kristy peered more closely at it, but couldn't work out what it said, or if it said anything at all. She sat back on her heels to think, and a beautiful, gold-framed mirror caught her eye. "That's it!" she exclaimed.

Kristy reached into her rucksack and felt around until her hand found a pair of sunglasses, mirrored ones. She pulled them out and held them near the floor so that their lenses reflected the stain.

"Wow!" Kristy gasped. Her guess had been right. The stain *was* writing: mirror writing. She read out loud, "Nineteen fifty-four DF." What did that mean? *1954 (DF)*. "David Follman!" Kristy cried. "He wrote this! That must be it."

Suddenly, she heard footsteps moving away from the doorway of the dining room. Someone had been watching her. She flipped the carpet back over the stain and ran out of the room, just in time to see Cary Retlin disappearing down the hall. Had he seen Kristy's discovery? She had no way of knowing. But she did know, for sure, that she'd found an important clue.

I werked with Ms. Coorton today. I am becoming fasinated by ar̶t̶i̶t̶c̶h̶ — ar̶c̶h̶i̶t̶e̶c̶t̶ — arcitecht — by what she does for a living. We found some very intresting blueprints today . . .

Claudia's entry described an afternoon she had spent working with Miss Cureton, going over old blueprints to check for any structural problems that might make renovations difficult or dangerous. They looked at plans for the main building, the golf clubhouse, even the garden shed. Miss Cureton took notes and gave Claudia a short lesson on how to read blueprints. "This is a door," she said, pointing to a mark on the plan. "And this is a window. I'd like to tear down this part of the wall," she pointed to another spot, "and enlarge the window, so the dining room would have a view of the gardens. But if you'll notice, there's a weight-bearing beam there, and we can't take that out, or the wall will collapse."

Claudia was impressed. "How do you learn to be an architect?"

"You spend a *long* time at college," answered Miss Cureton, smiling.

"Hmmm," said Claudia. "Maybe I'll just stick to being an architect's helper, for now." She pulled out another set of blueprints. They were stamped "Revision, 1957" in the bottom left-hand corner. "This one looks more like a landscaping plan," she said. "It shows all the gardens." She traced the lines on the plan. "What's this?" she asked, looking at a strange, geometric design. "Is that the maze?"

"Let me see!" Miss Cureton said. "I was told that all the blueprints for the maze had been lost in a fire. This is quite a find."

They pored over it together. "What's that square shape in the middle of the maze?" Claudia asked.

"You know, I have no idea," answered Miss Cureton. "I was just wondering the same thing. It's some sort of structure, obviously, but there's no indication of its purpose. How odd."

Claudia thought it was odd, too. That's why she wrote it up in the mystery notebook.

Well, I met a Stoney-brook celebrity today. But he didn't exactly receive the celebrity treatment at Greenbrook....

The day after Claudia found plans for the maze, I was helping Nikki tidy up the lounge when she had an unexpected visitor. A man and his wife—prospective members—had just left the lounge, and I thought Nikki and I were alone. Then I heard a cough. I turned to see our visitor. He was an older man, stooped and grey, carrying a stick with a silver duck's head on top. "Can I help you?" I asked, but he didn't answer me. He just made a louder hurrumphing sound.

The noise made Nikki turn around, and her jaw dropped when she saw the old man. "Armstrong!" she exclaimed.

"*Mister* Armstrong," he corrected her. "What's going on here?" He looked around with obvious distaste.

"We're redecorating," said Nikki simply.

Armstrong hurrumphed again. "What would your father say?" he asked.

Nikki didn't answer.

"I remember when belonging to this club *meant* something," said Armstrong. "They didn't let just anyone in, you know."

Nikki nodded, frowning. I had a feeling I knew what she was thinking.

"Haven't been inside the old place in over twenty years," mused Armstrong. "You don't mind if I look around, do you?"

"As a matter of fact, I do," said Nikki, folding her arms. "I don't think it's a good idea for you to be here at all."

Armstrong gave a tremendous hurrumph. "You're heading straight for failure and bankruptcy, young lady, if that's how you treat potential members."

"You will *never* be a member here," said Nikki, her voice rising.

"Er, Nikki?" I asked, stepping forward. "Do you know where the brass polish is?"

Nikki looked at me blankly for a second. Then she smiled gratefully. "I'll help you find it, Abby," she replied, "as soon as we've shown Mr Armstrong out."

"No need for that!" he said. By then he was red in the face. "I'm as good as gone." He stomped off, pounding the duck-headed stick into the floor at every step.

I looked questioningly at Nikki after he left, but she didn't seem to want to talk about what had happened, so we went back to cleaning. Still, I couldn't put Armstrong's visit out of my mind.

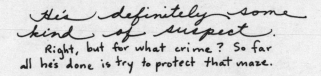

He's definitely some kind of suspect.
Right, but for what crime? So far all he's done is try to protect that maze.

Jessi and Mal weighed in with their own mystery notebook comments, about Mr Kawaja. They had spent an afternoon watching the children of some prospective members who were touring the club. While they played outside with the kids, they kept an eye on Mr Kawaja. They couldn't pin anything to him, but he was making them very, very suspicious, because of the way he guarded the maze and became agitated any time another person strayed near it. Mal was sure he was hiding something, and Jessi said he looked as if he had a guilty secret. But neither of them could work out exactly what Mr Kawaja might be up to, or how it might relate to the trail of clues we were following.

The mystery notebook was becoming crammed with notes and clues. But we couldn't put any of them together, and we weren't one step closer to solving the mystery of Dark Woods.

8th CHAPTER

"I think we'll concentrate on indoor jobs today," Nikki announced on Monday. The reason for her plan was obvious. It was drizzly, grey and cold outside. Several of us were gathered in the lounge, waiting to hear what we'd be doing that day. Alan Gray and Cary Retlin were there, and so was Cokie. The BSC contingent consisted of me, Stacey and Jessi. Stephen was there that afternoon, too. He was sitting on the sofa next to Nikki, looking bored.

"A couple of you," Nikki continued, "can help Mr Kawaja in the greenhouse, where he'll be starting seeds for some of the flowers we'll be planting this spring. Darcy needs a helper—" she broke off to smile at Cokie, who was waving her hand frantically, "—and I think she's found one. Also, I'll need a few people to be

75

'floaters', helping Miss Cureton and me throughout the afternoon."

Alan and Cary ended up with Mr Kawaja, Cokie (naturally) paired off with Darcy, and the rest of us volunteered to float. The rest of us, that is, except Stacey. She was too busy staring at the wall near the doorway to the lounge. I thought she was daydreaming, so I volunteered her. "What are you looking at?" I whispered, as the meeting ended and people began heading off to work.

"Wait a second, and I'll show you," she whispered back. We lingered in the lounge to give everyone else a chance to leave. Then, as soon as the room was empty except for us, she walked to the doorway and pointed to a crack between the doorframe and the wall. Sticking out of it, in a fairly obvious way, was a folded-up piece of paper. "I can't believe I never noticed this before," said Stacey. "I've been in this room plenty of times."

"The lights are on now, though," I pointed out. "Maybe they were never on before. Usually there's enough light from the windows, but it's pretty dark out there today."

"Maybe," she said. "Anyway, I'm dying to see what this is. Shall I?" She nodded towards the paper.

"Be my guest," I said, making a bow.

Using the edge of a hairclip she took out of her hair, she pulled out the paper and unfolded it carefully. I leaned over her shoulder, curious to see what the paper would reveal.

"What does it say?" I asked. The words on the paper were written in what looked like fountain pen ink, and while the paper was worn, the penmanship was so neat that it was easy to read the message.

"'The secret society exists. I have found it. The proof is near. The risk is great,'" we read together. Then we came to the last couple of words, and we slowed down. "'Think—*penguins*'?"

"Penguins?" I repeated. "What could that possibly mean?"

"I don't know," Stacey said, "but this looks like another clue from David Follman. It's even signed with his initials." Sure enough, at the bottom of the note were the initials "DF" in brackets, just the way they were written on the dining room flooring.

"Oh, it's definitely a clue," I said. "But penguins? How are we supposed to think penguins?"

"Let's show Jessi the note," suggested Stacey. "With all three of us working together, maybe we can work it out."

We went off to find Jessi, and discovered her in the dining room, hanging around with Stephen while Nikki made some phone calls. Jessi and Stephen were talking about the neighbourhood kids' club. "Mal said the plans are really coming along," Jessi said. "But I'm sure they could still do with more help. Laying out the miniature golf course is a pretty big job." I knew she had talked to Mal about how hard it seemed to be for Stephen to make friends. Now she was doing her best to help him along. But Stephen didn't seem ready to be helped.

"Maybe," he said doubtfully. He didn't look at Jessi.

"Listen," I said, thinking quickly. "We have a fun game to play today. How about if we try to find penguins—or anything like a penguin—on the club grounds?" I thought Stephen might be able to help us out, as he probably knew the club pretty well by now, but I wasn't sure if we should involve him in our mystery.

"Penguins?" asked Jessi, looking confused.

Stephen looked interested. "OK, I suppose," he said to me. "It sounds like fun. But I don't know where any penguins are."

While Stephen was talking to me, Stacey slipped David Follman's note to Jessi, who read it, raised her eyebrows, and then nodded.

78

"Well," I said, "maybe we just have to think of things that remind us of penguins. Like—like men in dinner jackets! Maybe those pictures in the hallway mean something. Let's go and see." I stood up to leave, and just then Nikki came into the dining room. "I need one of you in the kitchen," she said. "The worktops in there need a good scrubbing."

"I'll do it," Jessi volunteered.

"Check in the freezer," I hissed as she followed Nikki out of the room. "You know—ice? Penguins?" I knew it sounded ridiculous, but we had to follow every lead.

And that's exactly what we did, the rest of the afternoon. In between doing jobs for Nikki, the three of us, with Stephen's help, searched high and low, over almost every inch of that club, for anything even remotely resembling a penguin.

While I hoovered the hallway, I checked those old photos, and while some of the men in dinner jackets did look penguin-ish, no other clues came up there.

Jessi finished scrubbing the worktops, then poked around in the freezers (including the huge walk-in one) in the kitchen. They were empty. Not a penguin to be found.

Stacey braved the outdoors (Nikki had sent her to the garden shed with a message for Mr Kawaja) and checked around the fountain, which had statues of swans in it. "You know, swans, penguins. They're all birds, right?" she explained. But the swans weren't giving up any secrets, if they had any to give.

Near the end of the afternoon, Stephen thought of checking through some old nature magazines he'd seen in the lounge. It turned out that he was the only one of us who actually did find penguins, in an article called "Formal Friends of the Frigid Floes". The article was illustrated with pictures of mama penguins, papa penguins and baby penguins—thousands of penguins, looking like crowds of strangely formal little clowns. But there was no sign of any further clues left by David Follman. Stephen was excited by his find. It wasn't what we were looking for, but I congratulated him anyway and told him he'd won our game. Happy, he ran off to tell Nikki.

"I give up," said Jessi, after we'd each paged carefully through the magazine. She plopped herself down in an easy chair and sighed. "This is going nowhere."

I sat on the sofa opposite her. Stacey, in a rocking chair, pulled the note out of her pocket and stared at it one more time, as if she could force it to make sense.

Alan Gray poked his head round the

door. "Hey, everyone," he said. A little smile was playing around the corners of his mouth.

I think we were too discouraged even to wonder about what might be amusing him. "Hi, Alan," Stacey said tiredly.

Alan's grin grew wider. "Have a nice penguin search today?" he asked.

The three of us sat up straight and stared at him. "You!" Jessi cried.

"Did you write that note?" I asked.

Alan shook his head, still grinning. "Nope," he said.

"But how—" Jessi began.

"Hold on a second," Stacey said suddenly. She still had the note in her hand, and now she held it up to the light and stared at it again. "OK, Alan," she said. "You may not have written this note. But David Follman definitely didn't either. This note was written recently."

"How do you know?" I asked. I leaned over to take another look at the paper.

She held it up again and pointed to something at the bottom of the paper. It was a watermark—the nearly invisible mark that manufacturers make on the paper. And the watermark on this paper included the "recycle" symbol, which hasn't been around all that long. "You're right!" I said. "So who did write it?"

Jessi, Stacey and I thought for about

three seconds. Then we looked at each other and nodded. It could only be one person. "Cary Retlin!" cried Stacey.

"Yes?" asked Cary, poking his head into the room. "You called?" He was smiling a devilish smile.

"Did you write this?" I asked, pointing to the note.

"Yep," he said, rocking back on his heels and smiling proudly.

"I bet you wrote those notes to Mary Anne and Logan, too, didn't you?" I asked, suddenly seeing a pattern.

Cary nodded and kept on smiling.

"But why?" asked Jessi.

"Complications make life more interesting," Cary said with a shrug. Then he tilted his head. "So how did you work out that the note wasn't really from DF?" he asked.

Stacey showed him the watermark. I could tell she wasn't happy to have been fooled, even for an afternoon.

"Good detective work," said Cary.

"Thanks," said Stacey, glaring at him. "And thanks for sending us on a wild goose—I mean, wild *penguin* chase."

That did it. We couldn't help cracking up. We were still furious with Cary, but now that it was over, we had to admit that the day had been kind of fun.

9th
CHAPTER

Tuesday

Well, the good news is that Stephen has figured out a solution to his problem — the problem of feeling left out, that is. The bad news is that I'm not so sure it's the best solution....

Stacey had read Mal's entry in the club notebook, so she wasn't surprised that afternoon when she arrived at the Stanton-Chas' and found Stephen lying on the sofa, sulking. His face was turned away from the window, as if to ignore the blue sky outside. It was one of those cool but pretty February days when you can begin to imagine spring arriving soon.

"He's in a bad mood," Nikki told Stacey as she left. In a lower voice, she added that Stephen was lonely, and missing his dad, who was still in Korea. "Please try to persuade him to play outside with some other kids," she said. "I hate to see him lie around inside, all alone."

Stacey sat down on the sofa near Stephen's head. "Are you feeling alright?" she asked him.

"Mmph," muttered Stephen. "Grrph."

"What's that?" asked Stacey playfully. "Did you say you needed to be tickled?" She gave him a little tickle, under the arms. An "experimental tickle," as she told me later, just to see if he felt like being cheered up.

Stephen squirmed, and Stacey thought she heard a tiny giggle. "Did you say something?" she asked, tickling under his chin.

Stephen rolled over and giggled louder. "That tickles!" he squealed.

"Good!" said Stacey, tickling his feet. "It's supposed to." Before long, Stephen was laughing out loud and tickling her in return. "Hey, how about if we go outside and play for a while?" she asked. She decided she wouldn't mention other kids yet. She'd wait and see how he felt about this first step.

"Play what?" asked Stephen warily.

"How about—how about Wiffle Ball?" Stacey suggested. She'd spotted a yellow plastic bat and a white ball in the entrance hall when she'd arrived.

"Will you pitch to me?" asked Stephen.

"OK," said Stacey. "Let's go!" She held out a hand and helped him off the sofa. They grabbed the bat and ball and went out into the garden. Stephen decided where home plate should be, and stood there, swinging the bat, while Stacey pitched to him. She threw about twenty pitches. Stephen swung at every one, and hit a lot of them, enough to keep Stacey running after the ball.

Finally, just as Stacey was winding up for another pitch, Stephen threw down the bat. "I'm bored," he said.

"Want to go for a walk?" asked Stacey. She didn't mention a destination, even though she had one in mind.

"OK," replied Stephen with a shrug.

A few minutes later, Stephen and

Stacey were standing on the pavement in front of the Pikes' house. They could see through the hedge that the side garden was full of kids: Nicky and the triplets, Vanessa, Matt and Haley, Charlotte and Becca, Jake, Carolyn and Marilyn.

The garden had been transformed. A big banner hung across the Pikes' old swing set, announcing (in every colour of the rainbow) the grand opening of the "Slate Street Kids Club".

Jordan, Adam and Byron were tossing around a Nerf basketball, aiming at a home-made hoop they'd fixed on one side of the garage. As they played, Jordan gave a running commentary, sportscaster-style. Stacey and Stephen could hear him loud and clear from where they stood. The funny thing about his narration was that everyone in the game had the same last name, so it sounded as though one incredible player was all over the court: "Pike pivots, takes the lay-up—but Pike blocks the basket. Pike passes to Pike, who dribbles to the three-point line, sets up, and—oooh, Pike steals the ball!"

Nicky and Matt were in the drive nearby, playing handball against the garage door. Carolyn and Marilyn were playing badminton (with ancient rackets and an old tennis ball instead of a shuttlecock) on a court set up behind the swing set. There was no net, just a piece of string that ran from the swing set to a tree. And Jake, Charlotte, Vanessa, Margo, Haley and Becca were in the middle of a round of miniature golf.

"I can't believe you made a hole-in-one!" Charlotte cried as Haley grinned and lifted her putter (actually a furled umbrella) over her head. They were near the third hole (each hole was marked by a little paper flag with a number on it), which had a teddy bear motif. Then Vanessa took a shot at the hole, and her ball flew past it. She stamped her foot. "That's my fifth shot!" she said. "Golf is fun? *Not!*"

Vanessa even rhymes when she's angry.

Jake, Margo and Becca took turns at the fifth hole, which was a watering can turned on its side. The path to the hole wandered through Mrs Pike's flowerbed. Stacey wondered how happy she'd be about that once the plants started to come up in the spring.

"They look like they're having fun, don't they?" she asked Stephen.

He nodded. "More fun than I have at Greenbrook," he said enviously.

"So what are you waiting for?" Stacey asked. She gave him a little shove. "Go and play with them."

Stephen smiled up at her. "I think I will!" he said.

For once, Stacey said, Stephen seemed eager to join the other kids, who looked as if they were having a terrific time. Stacey congratulated herself as she watched Stephen march up the Pikes' drive. At last he was on his way to making some new friends.

Then something awful happened.

"What are you doing here?" Nicky demanded, standing in Stephen's way with his arms folded across his chest.

"I—I just wanted to play," said Stephen.

"Well, you can't," said Nicky firmly. "Not until you've been invited to join the club. It's members only, you know!"

Stephen's mouth opened and closed, but no sound came out. Then, before Nicky or anyone else could say another word, Stephen turned and stalked off, passing right by Stacey as he walked away from the Slate Street Kids Club.

Stacey couldn't believe her ears. How could Nicky have been so unkind? That wasn't like him. She watched, stunned, as Stephen strode towards the pavement. Then she turned to look at Nicky, who was shrugging his shoulders as he talked to Adam.

There was nothing to be done about it,

at least not then. Stacey hurried to catch up with Stephen, who was walking quickly. She couldn't work out what on earth to say to him to make him feel better.

Luckily, she didn't have to say anything. Just as she caught up with him, Stephen passed by the front of the Pikes' house. Sitting on the steps were Claire Pike and Jenny Prezzioso. Jenny, who's four, lives near the Pikes. Both little girls looked glum, but when they saw Stephen and Stacey they waved and called them over.

"What are you two doing?" asked Stacey when she and Stephen (who was still not speaking) had joined the girls.

"Just sitting," said Jenny.

"We're not allowed to play in the garden," complained Claire.

"Why not?" asked Stacey. "Did your mum tell you to stay here on the steps?"

Claire shook her head. "No, she said we could play. But Nicky and Vanessa said we couldn't."

"They said we're too little," Jenny said.

"They said we're pests," Claire added. "And that we can't join their club."

"Stupid club," Jenny said. "Stupid, stupid club." She looked as if she were about to cry.

"Who needs their club?" declared

Stephen suddenly. "They wouldn't let me join either, just because I'm not like them. Let's start our own club! It'll be much, much better than theirs, and when they ask us to let them join, we'll say no."

Claire and Jenny gazed up at Stephen, awestruck. Was this older boy really serious? "Can we do that?" asked Claire.

"Why not?" Stephen replied. "I know all about clubs. My mum runs one."

"Wow!" breathed Jenny.

"Can we all go back to my house and start working on it?" Stephen asked Stacey.

"If you're sure that's what you want to do," answered Stacey hesitantly. Somehow the plan didn't sound so wonderful to her. She wasn't convinced that Stephen's background had anything to do with his being barred from joining the older kids' club, and she wasn't crazy about the idea of yet another exclusive club starting up. But at least Stephen would be playing with other kids. That was the goal, wasn't it? She went inside to arrange things with Mrs Pike (who said she'd phone Mrs Prezzioso), and when she came back she found Stephen, Claire and Jenny talking excitedly about plans for their club. Stacey had never seen Stephen look so happy. Maybe things would work out after all.

10th CHAPTER

"Hidden passageways, maybe. Secret trapdoors, definitely. But penguins?" Claudia giggled and popped another sweet into her mouth. "I can't believe you lot spent the whole day looking for penguins!" Her giggles escalated until she was laughing out loud.

Kristy, sitting in the director's chair, joined in. "I can just see it," she said. "A Nancy Drew mystery called *The Puzzle of the Purloined Penguin*!" She could hardly talk, she was laughing so hard. Mal and Mary Anne laughed along with her.

It was Wednesday, and we had just finished a BSC meeting. We'd all agreed to stay a little late in order to talk about the Greenbrook mystery—but first, it seemed, our friends needed to make fun of Jessi, Stacey and me for doing exactly what they would have done in our place:

91

following up a lead. The three of us just sat there, watching the rest of them laugh at us.

Finally the laughter started to become contagious. I couldn't help myself. I giggled a little. Then I noticed that Jessi was cracking a smile, too. Stacey raised her eyebrows and grinned. "Formal Friends of the Frigid Floes!" she said. That did it. We totally lost it.

"One day I'm going to give Cary Retlin a taste of his own medicine," vowed Stacey.

"I'll help you," I promised. "Whatever it takes, I'll help you."

"I wish you both luck," Kristy said. "Meanwhile, may I point out that we still have a mystery to solve here?" Suddenly she was Miss Chairman again. You'd never have known, from looking at her serious face, that she'd been laughing— laughing so hard she'd had to wipe away tears—only moments before.

"Right, right," agreed Stacey. "OK, who has the mystery notebook? Let's go over what we have so far."

"Here it is!" said Claudia, picking it up from her desk. "And, hey! Here are some Twizzlers, just to give us that extra mystery-solving energy boost." She passed around the packet she'd found under the notebook, and handed Stacey a bag of pretzels she dug out of her desk drawer. Then she opened the notebook and rifled through the pages until she found what she was looking for. "Well, we've written a lot down," she said, "but I'm not sure how much of it means anything."

"Let's go over it," said Kristy. "What do we have in the way of leads and clues?"

"Let's see," said Claudia. "First of all, there are the notes that Abby and Mary Anne wrote up when they heard about David Follman from Sergeant Johnson."

"That wasn't necessarily the first time we sensed there was a mystery, though," I said thoughtfully. "I had a feeling there was something weird about Greenbrook —or, about Dark Woods anyway—from the very beginning."

"I thought so, too," said Mary Anne, nodding and twirling a Twizzler absent-mindedly.

"Go on, Claudia," Stacey urged her. "What's next?"

"Well, Mary Anne and Abby also wrote up what Dawn's Granny and Pop-Pop said about Mayor Armstrong. He sounds like a definite bad guy, and he was pals with Mr Stanton, another of our possible suspects."

I shuddered, thinking about Armstrong, and his stick with the silver duck's head on top. He was a creepy old man.

I'd got a bad vibe from him. It wasn't hard to imagine him keeping Jewish people—people like *me*—out of a club. But could he really be responsible for covering up a secret society, and for murdering a journalist who was about to reveal it?

Suddenly I realized that this was serious business we were sticking our noses into. After all, somebody had wanted to shut David Follman up, and he (or she) had succeeded. David Follman would never be able to write about what he knew. But maybe, if we could just stay on the trail, my friends and I could finish the job he'd started. I leaned forward. "What else, Claud?" I asked. "Go on."

Claudia read little bits from the notebook out loud. We listened and nodded as she reminded us about the way Mr Stanton had been lurking around watching Stephen, and about the mysterious structure Claudia had spotted on the blueprints of the maze. That last part seemed to fit in somehow with what Mal and Jessi had written, about how Mr Kawaja seemed overly protective of the maze.

Claudia also read my notes about Nikki's unpleasant encounter with Armstrong. "I hope he never turns up again," I said. "He and his stick can just stay away, as far as I'm concerned."

"Sounds as if Nikki's not too thrilled about having him around, either," commented Jessi.

Finally, Claudia read to us from Kristy's notes about finding David Follman's scrawled message, in mirror writing, on the floor of the dining room. Then she snapped the notebook shut. "That's all," she said.

"That message is our only real clue, isn't it?" asked Mal. "We have to follow up on it."

"But how?" asked Stacey. "I mean, all it says is a number. If it's a date, it's not one that makes sense. It's years and years earlier than the time David Follman was doing his investigation. What could it possibly mean?"

"I'm thinking, I'm thinking," said Kristy, holding her head in her hands.

"What I don't understand is why he didn't just use a pen," said Mary Anne. "I mean, if you want to write a note, isn't that the easiest way?"

"For that matter, why did he write on the floor?" asked Jessi. She shook her head.

"We-ell," I said slowly. "Where else could you be sure of leaving a lasting message? Nobody ever looks underneath the carpeting." I thought I was beginning to see how David Follman's mind worked.

"OK, I'll buy that," said Kristy. "But what did he use to write with, and why did he choose it? It wasn't blood, because that would have turned brownish, and the stain is more purpley-red. Maybe it was something he found in or near the kitchen or dining room."

We nodded. Each of us had sneaked into the dining room at one point or another to check out the stain, so we all knew what it looked like.

"Let's be scientific about it," said Claudia, brightening. "I mean, when I want to create the perfect blend of colours for a painting, I experiment. It's the only way." She jumped up. "There's some leftover wooden flooring in the garage. We can try writing on it with different liquids and see what looks closest."

"Good thinking," said Kristy admiringly.

We went down to the Kishis' kitchen, rolled up our sleeves, and began our scientific experiment. It was a relief to be doing something instead of just talking about it, and, I have to admit, it was *fun*.

We arranged the planks of wood on the worktop and started to work. We tried red and blue food colouring. We tried cherry-apple juice. We tried cranberry sauce. We tried ketchup and spaghetti sauce. We tried every red or purple fluid in the

Kishis' kitchen—but nothing looked quite right. After a while, the wood started dripping. There was hardly any empty space left on it. And it smelled disgusting.

"It's lucky my parents are working late," said Claudia, glancing at the clock. "But they'll be home any second now. We'd better clean this mess up."

"Let me just try one last thing," I begged, holding up a bottle of grape juice. I drizzled some onto the plywood and rubbed it in. We looked at it hopefully, but then I shook my head. "Nope," I said. "It's not right."

Discouraged, we cleaned up the Kishis' kitchen and went home. I ate dinner and started my maths homework, trying my best to put the mystery out of my head for a while. Then, at around eight-thirty, the phone rang. It was Claudia.

"Abby, listen," she said. "That grape juice stain? You should see it now that it's dry. It looks a *lot* like the writing on the dining room floor."

"It does?"

"Definitely. And you know what else? I remembered something I saw on those blueprints. Guess what's right under the dining room?"

I had no idea. "The boiler?"

"Nope," said Claudia. "The wine cellar." She paused for a second to let that sink in. "Think about it, Abby," she said. "Wine is really just grape juice, isn't it? Maybe David Follman was trying to tell Sergeant Johnson to look in the wine cellar—"

"For a 1954 wine!" I finished excitedly. "Claud, you're a genius! Let's phone everybody else. We have to check it out as soon as possible." I had a feeling Claudia was right. Maybe we were finally on our way to solving the mystery!

The next afternoon, when the van pulled up in front of Greenbrook, I jumped out and went straight to the dining room. We had worked out a plan during our journey from school. Claudia, Stacey and Mal followed right behind me. I ran past the office, hoping Nikki wouldn't see me. We weren't sure she'd approve of our plan, but we also knew we'd be helping her out if we solved the mystery. We'd check in with her as soon as we'd finished. As I passed the lounge, I thought I caught a glimpse of a man who looked like Stacey and Mary Anne's description of Mr Stanton. But when I looked again he had disappeared, and I was in too much of a hurry to stop and wonder what he might be doing at Greenbrook again.

"How do we get down to the wine cellar?" I asked Claudia, after we'd taken one more look at the clue on the dining room floor.

"If I remember right, there should be some stairs just inside the kitchen door," said Claudia, leading the way. Sure enough, a few seconds later we found ourselves in a dank, dim basement.

I sneezed. "This is a wide cellar?" I asked. "It looks like an ordinary basebet to be. Sbells like wud, too," I added, pulling my polo neck up over my nose in an attempt to keep from breathing in any more dust.

"Try that door," suggested Mal, pointing to a huge wooden door set into one of the walls. Claudia tugged on its handle, and the door swung open, revealing another dusty, cobwebby room, only this one was full of racks, and the racks were full of wine bottles.

"Let's work quickly," I said, sneezing. "I cad't stay dowd here log."

We split up, and, turning on lights as we moved, we searched through the racks, looking for wine from the 1950s. It didn't take long to find it. The wine cellar was well-organized.

"Nineteen fifty-one, nineteen fifty-three," said Mal, reading the years on the labels as she checked each bottle in the section we'd focused on. "Nineteen fifty-four! Look at this one!" She held a green bottle up to the dim light coming in through a small window. The maroon seal around the cork was broken.

"Let be see that," I said. Mal handed me the bottle, and I pulled my trusty Swiss Army knife out of my pocket. I remembered watching my mum open wine, back when she was at cookery school and taking a wine-tasting course.

"Wait!" said Stacey. "Should you really open that? I mean, old wines are expensive, aren't they?"

I shook the bottle. Something made a clunking noise inside. "I don't think there's much wine in here," I said.

"Go ahead and open it," Mal urged me. "How else will we find out what's inside?"

I looked around, and the others all nodded. It wasn't hard to pull the cork out of the bottle.

"Ugh!" said Claudia, backing away. "Smells like vinegar."

"Does it?" I asked. My nose was so stuffed up I couldn't smell a thing. "Well, thed, we bight as well pour it out. Baybe there's a dote idside it." I turned the bottle over and poured its contents into the floor drain. As I shook out the last drops, something clinked on to the floor. "What's that?" I asked. I knelt down to look. A faded yellow golf tee lay on the floor—a golf tee with a message scratched into it. I peered at it, trying to read the tiny letters in that dim light. Finally, I read it aloud to the others. "OPEN WWII (DF)." That's all it said. Another clue. But what could it possibly mean?

11th CHAPTER

That night, I slept with the golf tee under my pillow. I was hoping that somehow it would reveal its secrets to me as I slept— but no such luck. When I woke up, I looked at it again, and its inscription still meant nothing to me. The only thing I was sure of was that it was another real clue. There was no way Cary could have faked this one. That golf tee had been placed in the wine bottle by David Follman himself, and every time I looked at it my heart beat a little faster. I was positive we were closing in on the solution to the mystery of Dark Woods.

All we had to do was work out what OPEN WWII meant.

After thinking about it all night, I was convinced that the message was on a golf tee for a reason. I couldn't wait to go to Greenbrook that afternoon and start searching the golf clubhouse.

102

Kristy, on the other hand, was sure the WWII part of the message meant something. "We have to research World War Two," she said at lunch that day at school. "The message has something to do with that time in history and how it affected Stoneybrook. I'm sure of it."

As it turned out, we were both right. But it took a while for us to find that out.

As some of the BSC members (Stacey and Claud) agreed with me about the importance of the golf tee, and some (Mary Anne, Mal and Jessi) agreed with Kristy, we decided to split up into teams. My team would investigate at Greenbrook, and Kristy's would do research at the library. We both kept notes for the mystery notebook.

Here are some basic facts about World War II and how it affected Stoneybrook: First of all, the war lasted from 1939-1945, but the US wasn't fully involved until 1941. During the war years, Stoneybrook was pretty much run by its women, since almost all the men had gone to war. Many men died. There are three major war memorials in Stoneybrook, which list their names. We're going to check them out next.

Kristy's team spent a lot of time at the library, learning about Stoneybrook's part in the war. And my team spent a lot of time at Greenbrook's golf clubhouse, learning about, well, golf.

Want to know how many times a hole-in-one has been shot on the seventh hole? We can tell you. Want to find out about golf equipment from twenty years ago? We know it all. We even know how many lockers there are in the men's locker room (we counted). But we still don't know what OPEN WWII means.

"Can you believe these old outfits?" Stacey asked, holding up a pair of black-and-white checked plus fours.

"I love it!" said Claud, who had found a floppy hat to match.

"Fore!" I yelled as I tried out a swing with one of the golf clubs I'd taken off a rack. As golf is one of the few sports I know nothing about, I don't know what "Fore!" means. All I know is that people shout it when they're about to swing a club.

"Four what?" asked Claudia.

"Four tons of stuff to clean up," answered Stacey, looking around with a sigh.

104

We were in the pro shop, which was part of the golf clubhouse. Nikki had been thrilled when we'd volunteered to start cleaning it out. It was the one place in the club that she hadn't even begun to tidy up.

The clubhouse was in a small, one-storey building of its own, just beyond the main building. It contained a locker room and changing area, a small lounge and the pro shop, where equipment and clothing were sold. The weird thing about the pro shop—about the entire clubhouse, for that matter—was that nobody had touched a thing in it for twenty years. Like everything else at the country club, it had simply been closed down and left alone when Dark Woods went bankrupt. Other places, such as the dining room, had at least been opened and aired before we saw them. But the clubhouse had been sealed up tightly until that day.

There were still golf shoes lying on the benches in the locker room, and cigar ash in the ashtrays in the lounge, and price tags (low ones!) on all the old-fashioned clothing in the pro shop. The trophy cases on the walls of the lounge still had trophies for the club's annual tournament, the Dark Woods Open, plus awards for things such as Best Female Golfer and Most Improved Golfer.

The trophy cases and everything else in the clubhouse needed a thorough cleaning. And we wanted to investigate every square inch. But we'd decided to start in the pro shop.

I put down the golf club I'd been swinging and strapped on the white surgical mask I'd brought along. I wear one whenever I'm in a situation where it's impossible to avoid dust. If I hadn't had one on that day, I probably would've ended up in Casualty. No joke. It was seriously dusty in there. The counters were dusty, the clothes were dusty, even the cash register buttons were dusty.

The mask helped, but I was still feeling a little sneezy and stuffed up as I piled boxes of golf gloves into the container Nikki had given us. She'd asked us to store all the old stuff we found in the shop, to make room for new gear. She was going to try to sell all the old merchandise at a special "nostalgia" sale in the summer.

An hour or so later, I threw one last box into the container, folded the flaps closed, and taped them shut. Then I sneezed.

"Bless you!" Claudia and Stacey said, for what seemed like the fortieth time that day.

"Thanks," I said. I looked around. "We seem to be making headway in this

106

place," I said. "How about if we take a break and do some investigating?"

Stacey and Claudia agreed. We divided the shop into sections, and each of us searched our area, hoping to find clues. But there wasn't a clue to be found. The closest we came was when I discovered a box of yellow golf tees—tees that looked exactly like the one we'd found in the bottle of wine.

"This proves that David Follman bought that tee right here in this shop!" I exclaimed.

"Maybe, but don't all golf tees look pretty much alike?" asked Stacey.

"Oh. Right," I said. My only clue was a non-clue.

We kept searching, but nothing else turned up. We kept cleaning, too. We worked in that clubhouse for three afternoons, and by the time we'd finished with it, the place was starting to look terrific, but we hadn't come any closer to working out what OPEN WWII meant.

By the end of the three days, I was tired and a bit cranky. More than a bit cranky, actually, which is why I ended up having an argument with Alan Gray. And believe it or not, that fight ended up being the best thing that could have happened.

We were taking a break in the lounge of the main building: Cary and Alan (who had been helping Mr Kawaja again), Stacey, Claud, me, Kristy and Jessi. (Kristy's team was just as frustrated as ours. They hadn't found any more clues, either. They had ended up coming back to Greenbrook to help us out.) Mary Anne and Mal had sitting jobs, so they missed the excitement.

Anyway, there we were, trying to relax, when Alan and Cary started giving us a hard time about who had a tougher job. "Having fun over in the clubhouse while we slave away in the greenhouse?" asked Cary.

None of us bothered to answer.

"They probably just sit around all day in the lounge over there," said Alan.

"We do not!" I cried. "We work harder than you'll ever work. We've cleaned that stupid clubhouse from top to bottom!"

"Well, isn't that great!" said Alan, raising an eyebrow. "What do you want, a trophy?" He stood up. "Come on, Cary," he said. "We've rested long enough. Let's get back to work."

The two of them marched out, leaving me steaming. It's no fun to be told that you're lazy, especially when you've been working as hard as we had. "Those two!" I said, shaking my head. "What do you want, a trophy?" I repeated, mimicking Alan.

Nobody said anything for a few minutes. Then, suddenly, I sat bolt upright in my chair. "A trophy!" I exclaimed. "That's it!"

"That's what?" asked Stacey tiredly.

"Has anybody cleaned that trophy case yet?" I asked.

"I've dusted the outside of it, but that's all," replied Kristy. "Why?"

"I've just remembered what most of those trophies are for," I said. "They're for the Dark Woods Open." I paused to let that sink in, but none of my friends reacted. "*Open*," I repeated. "Like in David Follman's note. Don't you think that might mean something?"

Suddenly, everybody looked a little less tired.

"What about the World War Two part?" asked Stacey.

"Maybe—maybe he means to look at trophies won during World War Two," suggested Kristy.

"What are we sitting here for?" I asked. "Let's go and check it out!"

We raced to the golf clubhouse and stood in front of the trophy case. "Which years do we need to look at again, Kristy?"

She thought for a second. "Nineteen forty-one to nineteen forty-five, I suppose," she said.

There was only one trophy from the war

years, and it was from nineteen forty-two. The plaque on it read, "Honorably recognizing the triumph of Christopher Armstrong". I opened the case (fortunately, it was unlocked) and lifted the trophy out. My friends gathered around to watch as I inspected it, and when I turned it upside down, we heard a rattling noise.

It didn't take long to find the false bottom, and moments later we had opened the trophy to find two small silver keys and a note. With trembling hands, I unfolded the paper, and we read it together. "Shelter Favourite Food", it said. And it was signed (DF), just as the other notes had been. We stared at it, but nobody said a word.

Finally, Kristy spoke up. "I think it's time to talk to Sergeant Johnson," she said. "Maybe he can make some sense of this."

Sergeant Johnson scratched his head. "Beats me," he admitted. "I can't work it out." He was looking over the notes we'd brought him. We'd taken every piece of evidence to the police station, except for the trophy. (Kristy had copied the inscription into the mystery notebook.)

"We probably should have come to you sooner, when we found the first one," said Claudia. "But we were so excited. We thought we were about to solve the mystery! Instead, we just found a tougher clue."

"Maybe David did too good a job of covering his tracks," said Sergeant Johnson. "But he must have thought that *somebody* would know what he meant."

I reread the trophy inscription that Kristy had copied. ". . . the triumph of Christopher Armstrong," I mumbled to myself. "Armstrong. Mayor Armstrong—the only man left in Stoneybrook during the war years," I said, remembering what Dawn's granny had told us, and what Kristy had discovered about the war years in Stoneybrook.

Suddenly, I had an incredible idea. "Listen everybody," I said. "I have a plan!"

12th
CHAPTER

"Welcome to the Blue Ribbon Club!" Stephen ushered us into the Stanton-Cha back garden.

Before I could put my plan into action, I had responsibilities to meet. I had a babysitting job the next afternoon. Actually, I had a *co*-babysitting job. Kristy was sitting for Stephen, and I was sitting for Jenny. She and Claire were at the Stanton-Chas' for the afternoon.

The three of them had spent quite a few days together, planning and putting together their "country club". Now it was ready, and Kristy and I were their first guests. They'd made us wait in the front garden while they prepared to greet us.

"Blue Ribbon Club?" asked Kristy.

"That's its name," explained Claire. "And all the members wear blue ribbons. See?" She showed us a scrap of blue ribbon she had pinned to her shirt. Jenny was wearing one, too, and so was Stephen.

"We tried some other names, like the S.J.C. club—you know, for Stephen, Jenny and Claire—but they didn't sound right," said Stephen.

"Also we kept fighting about whose initial should be first," said Claire. "I thought C.J.S. sounded a lot better."

"But the club is in my garden!" said Stephen. He sounded ready to start arguing all over again.

"And it's a beautiful club, too," said Kristy quickly. "Just look at that sign!"

Her effort to change the subject succeeded. The kids ran to the sign, which they'd painted on a long banner of computer paper, and hung across the Stanton-Chas' garage. In huge blue letters, it said:

It was decorated with yellow stars and swirls of blue.

"I did the stars!" Claire said.

"I made all the clouds," Jenny added, pointing to the swirls.

"And I wrote the words," Stephen said proudly.

"Terrific job, you lot," said Kristy. "Now, why don't you show us around your club?"

"What do you want to see first?" asked Claire.

"You decide," I said. "We want to see it all."

The kids were only too happy to give us the grand tour. They showed us the volleyball/badminton court, the swingball area and the sandbox corner. ("For the *little* kids," Jenny explained seriously.) Claire demonstrated the pogo stick, and Stephen showed us a pair of stilts he was learning to use. There was a Nerf football and a Nerf basketball, a Frisbee and three or four different Koosh balls. There was even a shop-bought miniature golf course. "In the summer we'll have a paddling pool," said Stephen, "and we'll play Super-Soaker tag."

Kristy and I were impressed. This was a big step up from the Pike kids' homemade club. The outdoor toys and sports equipment were brand-new. Nikki had obviously indulged Stephen when she saw that the club was making him happy.

"Let's play!" said Stephen. He ran to the badminton court, picked up a racket, and waited for the others to join him.

"I don't want to play stupid old bad-mitten," complained Claire. "I want to play swingball." She ran to the swingball pole.

"Yuck!" said Jenny. "I hate swingball. Let's play Frisbee." She grabbed it. "Come on, you lot."

It was stalemate. Not one of them would give in to the others, and none of them could play their game by themselves. Kristy and I stayed out of it, not wanting to play favourites by joining one game or another. We stood near the tall evergreen hedge that borders the Stanton-Chas' garden, watching the kids to see what they would do next.

"Wow!" I heard a voice whisper behind me.

"Awesome!" hissed another voice. "Look at the swingball."

"Real badminton rackets!" said someone else.

I turned around, peeped through a hole in the hedge, and saw Byron, Jordan, Haley, Nicky and Carolyn standing on the other side, staring into the Stanton-Chas' garden.

"What are you lot doing here?" I asked.

"Shh!" said Nicky. "Not so loud. We're spying."

"Spying?" asked Kristy. "Why?"

"Claire's been blabbing about her stupid club all week," explained Jordan.

"We wanted to see if she was telling the truth," added Byron.

"I think she was," said Carolyn, a little mournfully. She gazed longingly at the swingball game. "It really does look like a pretty cool club."

"Look at those stilts!" said Nicky. "I've always wanted to try those." Suddenly, he squirmed through a small opening in the hedge and ran into the Stanton-Chas' garden. The other kids looked at each other in surprise—and then followed him in.

"Hi, Claire," said Nicky cheerfully. "Nice club."

Claire put her hands on her hips. "Thanks," she said. "But why are you here?"

"Er," said Nicky, backing away a few steps. "We were—we wanted to—can we join your club?"

"Huh!" said Jenny, mimicking Claire's hands-on-hips pose.

"You must be joking," said Stephen, who was now standing between the two girls. "No way are you invited to join our club." He waved his hand around at the equipment in the garden. "All of this is ours, and you can't play with it."

Nicky stuck out his lower lip and glanced one more time at the stilts. For a second he looked as if he might burst into tears. Then he caught sight of his brothers and pulled himself together. "Well, you still can't join our club, either," he said. "So there."

"Who needs your silly old club, anyway?" asked Claire. "Ours is much, much better."

"Of course it is," Byron said, "if you like playing with a load of little babies."

"Babies!" yelled Stephen. "Take that back!" He clenched his hands into fists. "We're not babies. Our club is the best. And only certain people can join." He picked up the stilts Nicky had been eyeing, and started trying to walk on them, but he had a hard time, without help.

Claire ran to the swingball pole and smacked the ball. Jenny threw the Frisbee in the air and tried to catch it. "This is fun!" she cried.

"So is this!" said Claire, hitting the ball wildly.

"These stilts are the *best!*" called Stephen, just before he tumbled off them.

The other kids just stood with their arms folded, watching enviously. Then Byron seemed to pull himself together. "Hey, forget this," he said. "We have our own club, and it has the best members— not just little kids, like this one does. Let's go back to the Slate Street Kids Club!"

He stalked out of the garden, and the others followed him.

Nicky paused long enough to stick out his tongue at Claire. "Nyah, nyah!" he taunted her. "Who needs your baby club?" But I noticed him taking one last, lingering look at the stilts.

"Goodbye and good riddance!" shouted Stephen.

The Slate Street kids walked out of the garden and down the street. Stephen, Claire and Jenny stopped pretending to play and just stood there, looking a little lost. Suddenly the Stanton-Chas' garden was very, very quiet. And suddenly I couldn't take it any more. Neither could Kristy. We both started talking at once.

"Why wouldn't you ask them to join?" said Kristy.

"This is so silly!" I burst out. "You have equipment but you need more members—"

"—and they need more equipment but they have plenty of people," Kristy finished. "What's the point of being so exclusive?"

Stephen, Claire and Jenny looked upset and bewildered. "I don't know," said Stephen. "They wouldn't let me join, so I didn't want to let them join."

"Nicky can be quite fun to play with," Claire ventured.

"I like Carolyn," said Jenny. "And I bet Adam and Jordan would play Frisbee with me."

"I wouldn't really mind having a few more members," admitted Stephen.

Kristy and I exchanged glances. "I'll go after them!" I said. I dashed out of the garden.

I ran as fast as I could, and by the time I caught up with the Slate Street kids I was breathing hard, but I managed to gasp out my message. They followed me back to the Stanton-Chas'.

Kristy gathered everybody together near the tetherball pole, and started to talk—about including and excluding people, and about how Dark Woods used to be, and why Nikki wanted Greenbrook to be different. The kids seemed uncomfortable, but they were all listening. A couple of them looked extremely upset when Kristy told how Nikki's friend had been treated.

"That's so unkind!" said Adam.

"How stupid," agreed Margo.

"So tell me," Kristy said finally, to Nicky and the others. "Why didn't you want Stephen and Claire and Jenny to join in the first place? Did you have a good reason?"

Byron squirmed a little. "Claire and Jenny were being real pests that day," he said. "We were busy, and they kept annoying us."

"What about Stephen?" I asked. I was almost positive that it had nothing to do with his Korean father, but I had my fingers crossed behind my back, hoping against hope that I was right.

"We just didn't know him," said Nicky, shrugging. "I was going to invite him anyway, but he stomped off before I could."

"I wasn't even sure of his name," Jordan said. "But you seem nice," he added, addressing Stephen. "I know Claire's been having fun over here. She talks about you all the time."

"So, how about joining the clubs together?" asked Kristy.

"It's OK with me," Stephen said shyly. He was still glowing from what Jordan had said.

"Cool!" said Nicky. "Can I play with the stilts now?"

"OK," said Stephen. "And maybe later I can give you a karate lesson."

"Karate?" Nicky repeated. "Awesome! This club is going to be the best ever."

Kristy and I smiled at each other over the kids' heads. It looked as if the Slate Street Blue Ribbon Club was going to be a success.

13th CHAPTER

"Back off! Back off right now, or—or something might happen to the boy!"

I couldn't believe my eyes. Or my ears. I pinched myself, wishing that what I was seeing was just a nightmare. But I was wide awake, and I was horrified. This was not the way my plan was supposed to work out. How could everything have gone so wrong?

It all began a couple of days after my friends and I had gone to see Sergeant Johnson. We had put the little silver keys and the note back into the false bottom of the trophy, and returned the trophy to its place in the golf clubhouse. Then we were ready to put my plan into action.

Here's what I did next: I sent a letter to former mayor Armstrong. And it wasn't a "Hi, how are you? I'm fine" type of letter. It was an anonymous letter, accompanying a note that had supposedly just turned up, a note from David Follman to Sergeant Johnson (which I had really written). A note which said that Follman had "found the goods on Armstrong" and that Johnson should look in Armstrong's golf trophy for the key to the mystery. The letter went on to suggest that Armstrong might be interested in what else the note had to say.

Where had the note come from? No, I hadn't found it at the club. It was a forgery. I'd written it myself. (I suppose I have to give some credit to Cary Retlin for the idea.) You see, I had a hunch that Armstrong might know what David Follman's "Shelter Favourite Food" note meant, and that he'd lead us to the answer, incriminating himself in the process. By the end of the day, we would know the answers to the mystery of Dark Woods. It was all supposed to work out very neatly.

But something had gone terribly wrong.

It had started out perfectly. All the BSC members were at Greenbrook, and so was Sergeant Johnson. Stacey was sitting for Stephen at the club. The rest of us were ready for action. I had filled Nikki in on the plan, and she was eager to help. She had sent a gracious note to Armstrong, apologizing for being rude and inviting him back to Greenbrook for a tour of the club. He accepted immediately, no doubt because he was curious about "Follman's" note, and couldn't wait to follow up on it.

At first, everything went exactly according to plan. Nikki led Armstrong around the club on a tour. We BSC members, together with Sergeant Johnson, followed them, being ultra-careful to stay out of sight. (We must have made quite a sight: a tall policeman and a line of girls, all tip-toeing around.) First, Nikki showed Armstrong the main building, explaining the renovations in great detail (I think she enjoyed torturing him a little, as she knew he was dying to get at that trophy). She even showed him every single swatch Darcy had gone through before she'd chosen the "perfect" material for the dining room curtains. Then she took him over the grounds, telling him about what flowers would be blooming in each month of the summer. She showed him the newly resurfaced tennis courts, and the new changing rooms near the pool. Then, finally, she led him to the golf clubhouse and showed him around in there, explaining the planned renovations. We followed quietly, staying hidden every step of the way. We could see and hear them, but they couldn't see us.

"You probably feel most at home here," Nikki said at one point, when they were both standing near the trophy case. "Hardly anything's been changed yet."

Armstrong nodded and smiled, but he kept glancing nervously at the case.

"I think that's about it for our tour," Nikki said, just as we'd planned. "I need to go back to my office. But you're very welcome to relax in the lounge here. You'd probably like to sit and reminisce for a few minutes."

Armstrong agreed—very eagerly—and thanked her for the tour. Then he watched Nikki leave. I held my breath and crossed my fingers, but I didn't have to wait long before he did exactly what I had predicted he would do. As soon as he heard the clubhouse door close behind Nikki, he headed straight for the trophy case.

He put down his stick and opened the glass door. Then he gave one quick glance around (we all ducked down behind the sofa we were peering over), and pulled out a trophy. Fumbling a little, he unscrewed the false bottom and shook out the keys and the *real* note from David Follman to Sergeant Johnson—the one that said "Shelter Favourite Foods". As he unfolded the note, his hands were

124

shaking so hard that I could see the tremors from where I was hiding. I could also see that his forehead was glistening with sweat, and I could have sworn I heard his heart pounding.

My own heart was beating pretty fast. This was the moment of truth. Would he know what the note meant?

He read it quickly and wrinkled his brow, and then he read it again. He glanced at the silver keys he held in his palm. Then he read the note again. I felt my heart sink. Obviously, he wasn't sure what the note meant. Was my plan ruined?

Suddenly, a purposeful look came into Armstrong's eyes. He grabbed his duck-headed stick and, pocketing the note and keys, turned and walked off quickly, towards the back door. He never even glanced towards our hiding place behind the sofa.

"Yess!" I said under my breath. "Let's go, troops." I motioned to the others, and we followed at a safe distance.

Armstrong went out of the door of the clubhouse and straight towards the gardens. "Where's he going?" hissed Sergeant Johnson. I shrugged. I was as curious as he was. We just kept following the man with the stick.

It didn't take long for him to reach his

destination. Where was he going? If you guessed, you're a better detective than I am.

The maze.

I should have known. There was something mysterious about that maze from the very beginning, and we'd all known it. But somehow I never guessed that it held the secret of Dark Woods.

Armstrong walked to the opening of the maze. I hurried, thinking he was going to disappear inside, but suddenly Mr Kawaja materialized and stood in front of the former mayor, arms folded. Mr Kawaja had a very obstinate look on his face.

"Oh, no. He's not going to let him in!" I hissed. I was standing behind one of those huge bushes I'd helped to prune. Sergeant Johnson was next to me, while Kristy, Claudia and Jessi crouched nearby, behind another bush. Mal and Mary Anne were hidden by a large tree.

I had a terrible feeling that things were beginning to go wrong. And then something happened that made me sure of it. While Armstrong was busy arguing with a silent but stubborn Mr Kawaja, Stacey came running up to me.

"Abby!" she whispered. "Stephen's missing!"

"Missing?" I asked. "What do you mean?"

126

"He ran off. I can't find him anywhere. And I'm almost positive I've seen Mr Stanton hanging around. I think Stephen may be in danger!"

Just then, out of the corner of my eye, I saw Armstrong shove Mr Kawaja aside and run into the maze. I thought fast.

"Sergeant Johnson and I have to follow Armstrong," I said. "The rest of you can start searching for Stephen in the gardens. Be careful!"

Sergeant Johnson nodded at me, and we took off. We ran past Mr Kawaja, who was still sprawled on the ground, and into the maze. Almost immediately, I knew we were in trouble. We ran through hedges that stretched over our heads, taking so many right and left turns that I knew there was no way I could retrace my steps. And then, the worst possible thing happened.

We ran into a dead end.

"Oh, no!" I cried. "We've lost Armstrong for sure."

Just then, Mr Kawaja appeared. "Follow me!" he said.

I was stunned. "You can speak?" I asked.

"When it's important, I speak," he answered seriously. "Follow me," he repeated. Then he turned and started walking fast.

Sergeant Johnson and I exchanged

looks. His said, "Can we trust him?" Mine said, "What choice do we have?"

We followed Mr Kawaja.

He led us through what seemed like fifty twists and turns in the maze. I was just starting to wonder if Mr Kawaja was purposely making sure we'd be lost, when suddenly we arrived at a wide open space: the centre of the maze.

And there, kneeling on the ground and clawing at the dirt, was Armstrong. His duck-headed stick was flung to one side, and he was so intent on his task that he didn't hear us approach.

I couldn't work out what he was doing until we came a little closer. When we were about five metres away, I saw it. A trapdoor. Armstrong was scrabbling in the dirt, uncovering a secret door.

Suddenly, I heard a rustling in the bushes, and Stephen popped into the clearing. What a relief! He wasn't lost after all. I started towards him, but Sergeant Johnson held me back.

"Armstrong!" said Sergeant Johnson. "Stop where you are!"

Armstrong looked up, surprised. His glance took in me, Sergeant Johnson and Mr Kawaja. Then he spotted Stephen, and in one move—a surprisingly strong, fast move for such an old man—he grabbed the boy and clutched him tight.

"Back off! Back off right now, or—or something might happen to the boy!" Armstrong shouted.

That's when I pinched myself, and discovered that I was definitely not dreaming. Sergeant Johnson laid a hand on my shoulder, as if to reassure me, and to hold me back. Then I heard another rustling in the bushes, and Mr Stanton appeared. I stared at him, shocked. Was he still part of Armstrong's crooked group? Was he here to save his friend? I started to say something, but Sergeant Johnson shushed me.

"We're going to move back a little," he told Armstrong. "Don't hurt the child."

Armstrong watched us move back. Then he turned to Mr Stanton. "Paul," he said warmly.

"Let go of my grandson," commanded Mr Stanton. "Now."

"But, Paul!" said Armstrong. "If I do that, then this gentleman," he nodded at Sergeant Johnson, "will come after me. You understand, don't you—brother?"

"I'm not your brother," said Mr Stanton, spitting out the words. "I never was. Let go of the boy, or I'll tell everything."

Slowly, Armstrong loosened his grip on Stephen. Mr Stanton knelt and held his arms open, and Stephen ran to them.

Then everything happened at once.

Sergeant Johnson sprang forward and handcuffed Armstrong to a small apple tree. He read him his rights. Nikki rushed into the opening, along with Claudia (who had had the brains to run and find the blueprints to the maze) and the other BSC members. Nikki joined her father and Stephen in a huge hug.

"I've been so stupid, Nikki," Mr Stanton was saying. "Can you forgive me? I've been watching Stephen and beginning to feel as if I know him. Then I saw him in danger, and I knew what a fool I'd been."

As my friends and I watched, Nikki hugged her father tighter. Obviously, all was forgiven. I heard Mary Anne sniff, and I couldn't blame her for crying. I was practically ready to cry myself, from relief. My plan had gone wrong, but in the end everything had worked out.

14th CHAPTER

Or had it?

There was no question that Stephen was safe, and that he and Mr Stanton were heading for a beautiful future as grandfather and grandson. I found myself becoming a little choked up as I watched them—and Nikki—leave the maze together, led by Mr Kawaja. I think they were so thrilled at their newfound closeness that they'd forgotten about Armstrong and the mystery of the secret society.

But I hadn't. Oh, maybe I'd put it out of my mind for a few seconds, but that was all. The scene being played out in the centre of the maze had been beautiful, but we still had a mystery to solve. And the first thing to do was to find out where that trapdoor led.

Just as I woke to that fact, I heard a tiny clinking sound nearby. Armstrong had dropped the two little silver keys on to the frozen ground. I pounced on them, ignoring the old man's glare. He looked uncomfortable and angry with his wrists handcuffed to the tree. The duck-headed stick lay on the ground where he'd thrown it, and he seemed sort of naked without it. "If you use those keys, I can't be responsible for what happens to you," he said in a threatening tone.

I was standing near Mary Anne, and I could actually hear her gulp when she heard that. But he didn't scare me. I had a feeling he was bluffing. He knew that soon we really would have the goods on him.

I held up the keys. "Anyone interested in finding out where these lead us?" I asked. I headed for the trapdoor, joined by my friends and Sergeant Johnson.

"I've worked it out," said Claudia, brandishing the blueprints she still carried. "It's a bomb shelter. That's what 'shelter' must mean, in Follman's note." She showed us a tiny symbol on the blueprint, a pinwheel shape. "The secret society must have built the shelter for their own use, back when everybody was worried about the Russians bombing us."

Kristy frowned. "I bet they wouldn't have let certain people down there, either," she said. "If the club was picky about members, think how strict they'd be about who was in their bomb shelter!"

As we spoke, Sergeant Johnson was busy trying to prise open the trapdoor, using a tool that had been hanging on his belt. Suddenly, he gave a loud grunt and sat back on his heels. The door had popped open—just a crack, but it was open.

I stepped forward, grabbed the handle, and pulled the door all the way open.

"Wow!" breathed Jessi, who was looking over my shoulder.

"Wow is right," I said. We were staring down a long, steep flight of concrete stairs. The staircase disappeared into the gloomy dark. I couldn't see where it ended, which gave me a creepy feeling. The rest of my friends clustered around to look.

"I think we should go down there," said Mary Anne doubtfully.

"Definitely!" said Kristy. But I noticed she didn't step forward.

I wasn't feeling all that eager to walk down those steep, dark steps myself. But we had to, if we wanted to solve the mystery of Dark Woods. I took a deep breath to calm my nerves.

Just then, Sergeant Johnson stepped forward. I suddenly realized that I had ignored the fact that he had nearly fallen when the trapdoor had opened, and I felt terrible. I could have at least given him a hand up. I blushed as I looked up at him, but he didn't seem upset. He peered down at the staircase.

"Maybe you should all wait up here," he suggested. "I'll check things out and make sure it's safe." He unhooked a torch from his belt as he spoke.

His offer was tempting, but only for a second. There was no way I was going to miss out on being there when the mystery was solved. I'd spent too much time on it for that. I also had to admit that Sergeant Johnson and his torch made the stairs look much less scary.

"I'd rather come, if that's all right with you," I said politely. What if he insisted on going alone?

"Me, too," said Kristy.

"I want to come," said Jessi. Mary Anne, Claudia, Stacey and Mal spoke up, too.

Sergeant Johnson smiled. "I should have known you'd want to see this thing through," he said. "You kids are troopers." He switched on the torch. "Let's go, then," he said. "Just watch your step—and stay behind me." He started down the stairs. I followed him, and the rest of my friends were right behind us.

With Sergeant Johnson's torch beam lighting the way, the stairs didn't seem nearly as frightening as they had from

134

above. Still, I was nervous about what we would find at the bottom.

It felt as if we walked down stairs for a long time. There was a damp feeling to the air, and I started to wonder if my asthma was going to start playing up. How far underground were we going?

Finally, Sergeant Johnson stopped, so suddenly that I nearly bumped into him. Jessi *did* bump into me, and Kristy bumped into her, and so on.

"Sorry!"

"Ooops!"

"Sorry!"

It took a moment for everyone to sort themselves out in the dark. Sergeant Johnson waited patiently. Then he said, "There's a steel door here. And it's locked. Who has those keys?"

"I have," I said. I dug into my pocket, pulled them out, and put them into his outstretched hand. He took them, and handed me his torch in return.

"Shine this on the keyhole here, would you?" he asked. I held the torch carefully while he put a key in and tried to turn it. It didn't move. I bit my lip. He tried the other key. It turned, and the door swung open!

I shone the torch ahead, only to see a short corridor and *another* steel door. "They weren't taking any chances with

strangers coming in, were they?" I asked.
This time, I didn't even wait to be told.
I just shone the torch on the keyhole. Sergeant Johnson used the first key to unlock
the door, and we stepped into the bomb
shelter.

I was still holding the torch, so I shone
it around. The room we were in was small,
but it was packed tight with supplies. A
makeshift table stood in the centre, surrounded by folding chairs. Every wall was
covered with shelves, and every shelf was
covered with everything you can imagine
needing if you were planning to survive
underground for more than a few days.
Every box was carefully labelled. There
were medical supplies in boxes with big
red crosses on them. There were sheets
and towels and pillows, leading me to
think that there was another room somewhere for sleeping. There were huge
drums that must have contained water or
some kind of fuel. And there were shelves
and shelves full of food in cans and jars
and cardboard boxes. Fortunately for me,
the room had been sealed so tightly that
there didn't seem to be much dust.

"Incredible!" said Sergeant Johnson
softly.

"Awesome!" Kristy agreed. "They
really had it all planned, didn't they?"

"I wouldn't want to have to stay down

here, though," said Mary Anne with a shudder.

"I don't know," said Claudia. "It could be kind of fun—for a day or two. After that, I'd start going bonkers."

"How are we ever going to search for clues down here?" asked Mal, which snapped us all back to the mystery.

"It won't be much of a search," said Sergeant Johnson. "I've been thinking about it, and I have a feeling I know what David meant by 'Favourite Food'. Can I have that torch?" I handed it to him, and we followed him as he walked to one of the food shelves and started to rummage around. It was only a matter of seconds before he said, "Ah, here we go." He handed the torch back to me and used both hands to lift a large tin canister from the back shelf.

"Ovaltine?" I asked, shining the flashlight on the label. "What's that?"

"It's more of a drink than a food," explained Sergeant Johnson. "But without a doubt, it was David's favourite, back when we were kids." I heard a sad note in his voice, and remembered that the DF whose clues we'd been following had been a real person, and a real friend. "He loved the stuff," Sergeant Johnson said as he unscrewed the lid. "Couldn't get enough of it."

The lid came off, and everybody

crowded around to see what was inside the canister. There, in the torch's beam, was the answer to our mystery, I was sure of it. A bundle of papers, a notebook. It wasn't much to look at, but I knew it would tell us everything.

And it did. We brought the papers up into the light, and with Armstrong sitting nearby, silently fuming, we read through everything. There were smudgy photocopies of blackmail notes and records of all kinds of extortion. The names, dates and places were all spelled out—with Mayor Armstrong's being the name most often mentioned. I didn't spot Mr Stanton's name anywhere, which made me happy.

There was also a little red reporter's notebook, with the initials DF on the front. Inside we found a letter to Sergeant Johnson. He read it first, then handed it to me and turned away, but not before I saw the tears in his eyes. Here's what the letter said.

Dear Jim,
    Sorry about all I've put you through to bring you to this spot. I didn't mean to be dramatic. I just wanted to make sure my trail wasn't easy to follow. This evidence had to be safe where I left it.

If you're reading this, then I imagine things haven't worked out too well for me. They will have gotten to me before I've had a chance to publish this information. But I know if anyone can follow my trail to this — and bring the villains to justice — it's you. You are my best friend, and always will be.

David

15th
CHAPTER

It was a Saturday afternoon, not long after that dramatic scene in the bomb shelter, and my friends and I had a very important event to attend: the Grand Opening of the Greenbrook Club.

Even though it was only a few weeks later, it seemed as if what had happened that day in the middle of the maze had taken place in another lifetime. Instead of dreary grey, the sky was a perfect blue, with puffy white clouds sailing above. All along the drive and in front of the main building, bright yellow daffodils and red tulips were blooming cheerily in their beds. Spring had finally arrived, and even though I knew that meant allergy season, I didn't care. It also meant running, and softball, and being outside all the time. This was going to be my first spring in Stoneybrook, and I planned to enjoy every minute of it.

Starting with the biggest, best party of the season: Greenbrook's opening day. Nikki had invited everybody in town, it seemed. The place was packed with Stoneybrook dignitaries, kids and their parents, and athletic-looking people who were obviously itching to hit the tennis courts.

"This is terrific!" said Claudia, looking around as we entered the main building. She and Stacey had, naturally, dressed up for the occasion. Claud was wearing that old checked golf outfit she'd found in the clubhouse (which somehow looked up-to-the-minute cool on her), and Stacey wore a sparkling white tennis dress.

"Everything looks great," said Jessi.

"I can still smell the fresh paint," Mal said, sniffing.

"This club is going to be a success," said Mary Anne. "And Nikki deserves it, too. She's been working so hard."

"Look at the goodies!" said Kristy, leading the way to the buffet table, which was covered with delicious-looking treats. Then she spotted Alan and Cary, who had piled their plates high and were off to one side, stuffing their faces. "I suppose we're lucky you two left some for us," teased Kristy.

"We wouldn't have wanted you to go

hungry," said Alan, through a mouthful of cheesey puffs.

"Especially not after you did such a *great* job solving that mystery," added Cary with a grin. (All the SMS kids who were working at Greenbrook had heard about the mystery.) I couldn't tell whether he was giving us a sincere compliment or not. That's Cary for you.

"Well, thanks," I said, deciding to accept it as a compliment anyway. I grabbed a plate and started to fill it. But before I could even bite into my first egg roll, somebody grabbed my arm.

"Save some food for the *real* guests!" Cokie hissed into my ear.

At first, I was furious. I mean, who is she to tell me what to do? But then, when I turned to look at her, I forgot my anger and had to concentrate on not laughing out loud. Cokie, who had done her hair to look exactly like Darcy's, was wearing a dress that matched the maroon-and-cream colour scheme of the dining room.

"Nice upholster—I mean, dress, Cokie," I said, with a fake-polite smile on my face. "And, by the way, I *am* a 'real guest', and so are you. We all are, even though we worked here. Why else would Nikki have sent us those beautiful engraved invitations?" With that, I turned

142

and left her standing there with her mouth hanging open.

Plate in hand, I wandered around the room, just to see who was there. I noticed several of the prospective members I'd seen touring the club, and hoped their presence meant that they'd joined. Suddenly, I heard Stephen call my name. "Abby!"

I turned and saw him coming towards me, dragging a handsome Asian man behind him. "This is my dad," he said. He smiled proudly up at his father.

"Nice to meet you, Mr Cha," I said, shaking his hand.

"Nice to meet you," he answered. "From what I've heard, you and your friends have really helped Stephen begin to feel at home here in Stoneybrook."

He and I chatted for a few minutes, until we were interrupted by the arrival of Jake and Nicky, who were looking for Stephen. "Hey, dude!" called Nicky. "Great party!" He gave Stephen a high five. Then he turned to me. "Did you know that Stephen is Korean *and* American? Isn't that cool?"

I nodded and smiled. So did Mr Cha.

"This food is awesome," said Jake, displaying a plateful.

I saw Mr Cha smile. "Did Stephen tell

you about the Greenbrook Children's Club?" he asked me.

"I've heard a little about it—" I began, but I was interrupted by the boys.

"It's going to be so cool," said Nicky. "We'll have a whole room to ourselves, with Ping-Pong tables and games and everything."

"And we'll have swimming and golf and tennis lessons," Jake broke in.

"And a place for karate," Stephen added. "A real sensei—that means teacher—will be teaching, but I'll be his assistant."

"It'll be great to have our club here," said Nicky. "I mean, it was fun setting up those neighbourhood clubs, but setting them up was the best part. After that it was kind of boring."

"But with the club here, we'll meet all kinds of new kids," said Jake.

"Because anybody can be a member," Stephen finished, grinning at me. I smiled back. It was terrific to see him looking so happy.

After I'd wished the boys luck with the Children's Club and said goodbye to Mr Cha, I decided to take a look at the gardens. I was eager to see what kinds of flowers were coming up. I went outside and began to wander along the paths, looking at all the green shoots emerging from the dark, sweet-smelling ground. Then I spotted the bush we'd pruned on our second day at Greenbrook, but now I hardly recognized it. It was covered, and I mean *covered*, with brilliant yellow blooms. Looking at it just about took my breath away.

"Beautiful, isn't it?"

I whirled around and saw Mr Kawaja smiling at me. "It's forsythia," he told me. "My favourite spring bloom."

"I think it's my favourite now, too," I said, gazing at the way the blossoms stood out against the blue sky. We were both quiet for a moment. "Mr Kawaja," I said at last, "can I ask you something?"

"Of course," he said.

"Why were you so protective of that maze? Did you know about the bomb shelter? Were you trying to keep us away from it?"

He shook his head. "I had no idea the shelter was there," he said. "Those men must have built it the summer I was laid up with a broken leg." He paused. "No, the only reason I tried to keep you away was because I had to put so much work into that maze, and I did not want to see it damaged or destroyed. It means a lot to me."

"It's beautiful," I said.

"Thank you," he answered quietly. "I

hope many people will be able to enjoy it. I have promised Nikki that I will encourage anyone who wants to visit it." He turned to pick up the shovel he'd put aside. "And now I must go back to work," he said, giving me one last smile.

"See you, Mr Kawaja," I said. "I think I'll visit the maze now. I have a feeling I remember the way into the middle, and I want to check and see if I'm right."

"Have fun," he said, waving.

I made my way to the maze, and soon discovered that finding my way into the middle wasn't quite as easy as I'd thought. Still, after quite a few wrong turns and dead ends, I did eventually end up in the clearing in the centre. But I wasn't alone when I arrived.

Nikki and her father, Mr Stanton, had brought a rug and a couple of plates of food into the maze, and they were having a picnic in the clearing.

"Sorry to interrupt," I said.

"No, no, please join us," said Mr Stanton, moving aside so I'd have room to sit on the rug. "I've been wanting to talk to you and your friends, and thank you for helping to expose the dark past of Dark Woods, which is something I should have done long ago."

"Er, you're welcome," I replied. I didn't exactly know what to say. But Mr

146

Stanton didn't seem to notice. He kept on talking, as if he had to relieve himself of some terrible burden.

"Even though I was friends with Mayor Armstrong, he was never able to persuade me to join his society. I have struggled for years with those secrets," said Mr Stanton, looking down at his hands. Nikki reached out to touch his shoulder, and he smiled sadly at her. "I knew Armstrong and his cronies had done wrong," he continued, "but I didn't know how *much* wrong. Still, even though I held myself away from those men, Christopher was one of my oldest friends, and I couldn't turn him in. I kept quiet for so long—until I saw my grandson in trouble. Suddenly, keeping Armstrong's secrets meant nothing to me." He fell silent, and Nikki reached over to give him a hug.

"It's OK, Dad," she said softly. He hugged her back, and I began to feel self-conscious about intruding on their father-daughter reunion.

"I have to be going," I said. "I'm glad everything worked out," I added a little awkwardly.

"So am I," said Mr Stanton, gazing at Nikki. "So am I."

I found my way out of the maze easily, and sat down on a bench near the entrance, just to relax for a moment and enjoy the sun. I must have dozed off for a few minutes, because the next thing I heard was somebody telling me I looked "just like a cat snoozing in the sun".

It was Sergeant Johnson, and I was very happy to see him. I'd been wondering how everything had worked out after he took Armstrong back to the police station for questioning, and this was the first time I'd had a chance to ask. He was glad to fill me in.

"Armstrong confessed to everything," he said. "Even to rigging the brakes on David's car—although he insisted that he never meant to kill him. He just wanted to scare him." He stopped and shook his head sadly. "He'll be charged with assault, anyway, but after so long I'm not sure the charges will stick. Same with the charges against him for the blackmail and extortion. Even with Stanton testifying, Armstrong may not spend much, if any, time in jail."

"Does that bother you?" I asked.

He shook his head. "Not really," he said. "The facts are out in the open now, and I think justice has been done. Armstrong is an old man, and whether he goes to prison or not, he won't be starting any more trouble, I'm sure of that." He frowned ruefully. "Anyway, punishing Armstrong wouldn't bring David back.

It's too late for that. But I think David would be pleased to know that the mystery of Dark Woods has finally been solved. And I think he'd like knowing that you and your friends were the ones who did it."

He smiled at me, and I smiled back. Then we both closed our eyes and let the spring sun warm our faces. At last, the winter was over.

The Babysitters Club

Need a babysitter? Then call the Babysitters Club. Kristy Thomas and her friends are all experienced sitters. They can tackle any job from rampaging toddlers to a pandemonium of pets. To find out all about them, read on!

1. Kristy's Great Idea
2. Claudia and the Phantom Phone Calls
3. The Truth About Stacey
4. Mary Anne Saves The Day
5. Dawn and the Impossible Three
6. Kristy's Big Day
7. Claudia and Mean Janine
8. Boy-Crazy Stacey
9. The Ghost At Dawn's House
10. Logan Likes Mary Anne!
11. Kristy and the Snobs
12. Claudia and the New Girl
13. Goodbye Stacey, Goodbye
14. Hello, Mallory
15. Little Miss Stoneybrook ... and Dawn
16. Jessi's Secret Language
17. Mary Anne's Bad-Luck Mystery
18. Stacey's Mistake
19. Claudia and the Bad Joke
20. Kristy and the Walking Disaster
21. Mallory and the Trouble With Twins
22. Jessi Ramsey, Pet-Sitter
23. Dawn On The Coast
24. Kristy and the Mother's Day Surprise
25. Mary Anne and the Search For Tigger
26. Claudia and the Sad Goodbye
27. Jessi and the Superbrat
28. Welcome Back, Stacey!
29. Mallory and the Mystery Diary
30. Mary Anne and the Great Romance
31. Dawn's Wicked Stepsister

32. Kristy and the Secret Of Susan
33. Claudia and the Great Search
34. Mary Anne and Too Many Boys
35. Stacey and the Mystery Of Stoneybrook
36. Jessi's Babysitter
37. Dawn and the Older Boy
38. Kristy's Mystery Admirer
39. Poor Mallory!
40. Claudia and the Middle School Mystery
41. Mary Anne Vs. Logan
42. Jessi and the Dance School Phantom
43. Stacey's Emergency
44. Dawn and the Big Sleepover
45. Kristy and the Baby Parade
46. Mary Anne Misses Logan
47. Mallory On Strike
48. Jessi's Wish
49. Claudia and the Genius Of Elm Street
50. Dawn's Big Date
51. Stacey's Ex-Best Friend
52. Mary Anne and Too Many Babies
53. Kristy For President
54. Mallory and the Dream Horse
55. Jessi's Gold Medal
56. Keep Out, Claudia!
57. Dawn Saves The Planet
58. Stacey's Choice
59. Mallory Hates Boys (and Gym)
60. Mary Anne's Makeover
61. Jessi and the Awful Secret
62. Kristy and the Worst Kid Ever
63. Claudia's Freind Friend
64. Dawn's Family Feud
65. Stacey's Big Crush
66. Maid Mary Anne
67. Dawn's Big Move
68. Jessi and the Bad Babysitter
69. Get Well Soon, Mallory!
70. Stacey and the Cheerleaders
71. Claudia and the Perfect Boy
72. Dawn and the We Love Kids Club
73. Mary Anne and Miss Priss
74. Kristy and the Copycat
75. Jessi's Horrible Prank
76. Stacey's Lie

The CAFÉ Club

Make room for a delicious helping of the Café Club and meet the members; Fen, Leah, Luce, Jaimini, Tash and Andy. Work has never been so much fun!

1: GO FOR IT, FEN!
Fen and her friends are fed up with being poor. Then Fen has a *brilliant* idea – she'll get them all jobs in her aunt's café! Surely parents and homework won't get in the way of the Café Club...

2: LEAH DISCOVERS BOYS
Leah's got plenty to occupy her – there's the Café Club, homework and the Music Festival. She certainly hasn't got time for boyfriends... But when her music teacher starts picking on her, help arrives in the form of a surprisingly attractive *boy*...

3: LUCE AND THE WEIRD KID
Nothing's working out for Luce at the moment. Grounded ... with *purple* hair ... and now this weird kid's got her into deep trouble at the café...

4: JAIMINI AND THE WEB OF LIES

Sometimes Jaimini wishes she weren't so clever. Then her parents wouldn't want to *ruin* her life by sending her to a posh school away from her friends. But as the Café Club plot to save her, Jaimini meets Dom and begins to change her mind...

5: ANDY THE PRISONER

Andy's parents have gone away and forced her to stay with creaky old Grandma Sorrell ... and forbid her to work in the café! Andy's got to break out – and she knows *just* the friends to help her...

6: TASH'S SECRETS

Tash has a secret wish. She dreams of having a father again. So the Café Club set out to make her dreams come true... But Tash also has another secret *no one* must find out. Because if they do Tash is afraid she will lose her friends...

7: FEN'S REVENGE

Fen's having trouble with boys. Playing stupid, annoying pranks is one thing, but sabotaging an important cross-country race is going too far. Fen's out for revenge ... and the Café Club are right behind her.

Midnight Dancer
Elizabeth Lindsay

Ride into adventure with Mory and her pony,
Midnight Dancer

Book 1: Midnight Dancer
Mory is thrilled when she finds the perfect pony. But will
she be allowed to keep her?

Book 2: Midnight Dancer: To Catch a Thief
There's a thief with his eye on Mory's mother's sapphire
necklace – and it's down to Mory and Midnight Dancer
to save the day...

Book 3: Midnight Dancer: Running Free
Mory and Dancer have a competition to win. But they
also have a mystery to solve...

Book 4: Midnight Dancer: Fireraisers
There's trouble on Uncle Glyn's farm – because there's a
camper who loves playing with fire. Can Mory and
Dancer avert disaster?

Look out for:

Book 5: Midnight Dancer: Joyriders
Book 6: Midnight Dancer: Winners and Losers

*If you like animals, then you'll love
Hippo Animal Stories!*

Thunderfoot
Deborah van der Beek
When Mel finds the enormous, neglected horse
Thunderfoot, she doesn't know it will change her
life for ever...

Vanilla Fudge
Deborah van der Beek
When Lizzie and Hannah fall in love with the same
dog, neither of them will give up without a fight...

A Foxcub Named Freedom
Brenda Jobling
An injured vixen nudges her young son away from her.
She can sense danger and cares nothing for herself –
only for her son's freedom...

Pirate the Seal
Brenda Jobling
Ryan's always been lonely – but then he meets Pirate and at last he has a real friend...

Animal Rescue
Bette Paul
Can Tessa help save the badgers of Delves Wood from destruction?

Take Six Puppies
Bette Paul
Anna knows she shouldn't get attached to the six new puppies at the Millington Farm Dog Sanctuary, but surely it can't hurt to get just a *little* bit fond of them...